Introduction

> For me the struggle is not between Palestinians and Arabs. The fight is between those who seek peace and those who seek war. My people are those who seek peace. My sisters are the bereaved mothers, Israeli and Palestinian, who live in Israel and in Gaza and in the refugee camps. My brothers are the fathers who try to defend their children from the cruel occupation, and are, as I was, unsuccessful in doing so. Although we were born into a different history and speak different tongues, there is more that unites us than that which divides us.
>
> —Nurit Peled Elhanan, an Israeli Jewish mother from Tel Aviv whose 13-year-old daughter was killed by a Palestinian suicide bomber in 1997

I N THE 1980s few people thought they would live to see the end of the Cold War, the end of Apartheid in South Africa, or a united government in Northern Ireland. But in less than one decade, all these conflicts ended. The walls came tumbling down because the peacemakers kept hope alive and worked tirelessly to make peace possible.

Volunteers from Rabbis for Human Rights–Israel (RHR) help Palestinian farmers in the northern West Bank plant trees on land that is now stranded between the Wall and the Green Line.

Peacemakers from every nation are urging an end to Israel's occupation of Palestinian land and its systemic discrimination against Arab citizens of Israel, a bleeding, untreated wound inflicted in 1948.

The introduction to the first edition of *Steadfast Hope* was written in a spirit of guarded optimism. We believed the newly-elected President Barack Obama would bring fresh leadership and vision to the struggle for just peace in Israel and Palestine. Those hopes were dashed in December 2010 as the US announced it could not curtail Israel's illegal settlements. Peacemakers' hopes were delivered another blow when, on February 18, 2011, the Obama administration directed the US ambassador to

the United Nations to veto a Security Council resolution condemning Israeli settlements in the Occupied Palestinian Territories as illegal (the US was the only Security Council member to do so).

And yet, the pursuit of peace and justice in Palestine and Israel moves inexorably forward—without the assistance of the current administration and despite the United States' inability to be an "honest broker" in this conflict. Like other global peacemaking movements that have succeeded in the face of setbacks, the quest for peace, equality, and security for Israelis and Palestinians will succeed because justice, although delayed, cannot be forever denied.

Once again in the history of our fragile world, this is a day for peacemakers to stand up and be counted—this is the proposition to which this second edition of *Steadfast Hope* is dedicated. Since the Israel Palestine Mission Network first published *Steadfast Hope* in 2009, our burning desire to speak to the Church with the unvarnished truth about this painful conflict has been affirmed by IPMN's global partners. These peacemakers—Americans, Palestinians, Israelis, and others around the world—have not only a hunger to know and share the truth but also a deep commitment to bring a peaceful resolution to this six-decade-old struggle.

IPMN supporter and friend, author and issue-expert Mark Braverman, observes the growth of the grassroots movement demanding just peace in the Occupied Palestinian Territories—a movement encompassing secular society and religious communities in small farm towns and urban centers of the world. Braverman says, "When politics fail, broad grassroots movements arise to change the political wind and bring required change....The Church is called to respond to this urgent situation, to take a stand against it. And, the Church has been here before."

Mark Braverman is right. The Church has been here before, and it is now awakening to the truth that God is calling it to be there again. This second edition is possible because our peacemaking partners from other faith traditions have recognized the need to keep telling the *Steadfast Hope* story. It is the story of both Palestinians and Israelis who are genuinely striving for a just peace in the land the world calls holy. We believe that this holiness is made real as we faithfully respond to Christ's call to peacemaking so that all may be called the children of God.

This Jerusalem Palestinian family, like Palestinians in the West Bank and Gaza, has experienced worsening conditions during the years of the "peace process." In negotiations, Israel has historically demanded "compromises" that merely cement past injustices—territorial loss, loss of sovereignty, and denial of the rights of refugees. Another precondition designed to codify Palestinians' inferior status has been added by the Netanyahu government—recognition of a "Jewish" state Palestinians know to be inherently discriminatory.

David Young

The Gospel mandate for peacemaking

THERE CAN BE no stronger mandate for peacemaking than the sermon on the mount in which Jesus promises that peacemakers shall be called children of God (Matt. 5:9). The United Presbyterian Church (U.S.A.) gave life to this mandate in 1980 when the General Assembly adopted the groundbreaking confessional

document, *Peacemaking: The Believers' Calling*. In it the church proclaimed (p. 17):

"God wills peace, 'shalom': total well-being, wholeness, fulfillment, health, joyous harmony....Peacemaking involves the utilization of political processes for social healing more than merely the assignment of political priorities. The biblical grounding of these truths is very extensive [citing Psalm 85:8,10, Psalm 37:11, Isaiah 54:10-17, Zechariah 8:12, Colossians 1:1-19, James 3:16ff]...."

Swords into plowshares

Additionally (p. 19), "The classical biblical image for peacemaking is the turning of swords into plowshares as found in the words of Isaiah 2:4: 'God shall judge between the nations, and shall decide for many peoples; and they shall beat their swords into plowshares, and their spears into pruning hooks; nation shall not lift up sword against nation, neither shall they learn war anymore.' Faith, hope, and love enable believers to give plowmaking priority over swordmaking, not because such a strategy is more 'successful' but because believers are called to be peacemakers in the presence of enemies."

Peacemaking: The Believers' Calling has been endorsed by over 4,500 PC(USA) congregations over the past quarter century. It finds its grounding within the biblical and theological framework of an ongoing tradition of Presbyterian peacemaking.

A historic commitment to peacemaking

Even before 1980 a succession of General Assembly statements highlight the church's historic and consistent commitment to international peacemaking, beginning with a call in 1946 for the immediate cessation of the manufacture of atomic bombs. Other Assemblies issued statements in 1954, 1956, and 1962.

In 1969 the Assembly proclaimed that God is the Lord of conscience, not only of a participant in war for moral reasons, or the objector to all war on pacifist grounds, but also of those who conclude that a particular conflict is morally unconscionable.

And in 1970 it urged that in the absence of a declaration of a state of war..."all military combat by the United States armed forces in Southeast Asia be terminated."

The 187th General Assembly in 1975 affirmed that the maintenance of economic advantages to sustain a high standard of living is not and cannot be considered just cause for supporting or participating in war or military action on the grounds that such action is inconsistent with the life and teaching of Jesus and the faith of the church.

In adopting *The Believers' Calling* in 1980 the 192nd General Assembly affirmed peacemaking and declared: 1) The church is faithful to Christ when it is engaged in peacemaking; 2) The church is obedient to Christ when it nurtures and equips God's people as

A delegation of 22 people from San Francisco Bay Area Presbyterian churches worked in February 2008 with the family of Izzat Abu Latifeh, a Palestinian olive farmer whose fields are located near Jaba'a in the Bethlehem Governorate, West Bank. Here, a "bucket brigade" of delegation members unloads a truck carrying olive tree seedlings while others prepare the ground for planting.

Solidarity delegations give Americans direct experience with Palestinian life under occupation and personal encounters with Israeli and Palestinian peacemakers. On Harvest Delegations, participants assist and accompany Palestinian farming families who often face harrassment and violence from Israeli settlers attempting to disrupt the annual olive harvest. During this Planting Delegation in February 2008, Palestinian olive farmer Izzat Abu Latifeh explains to Carl Basore of the Redwoods Presbytery how to plant a two-year-old olive tree seedling in rocky soil. In one day, delegation participants planted over 300 olive trees.

Richard Schlobohm

peacemakers; 3) The church bears witness to Christ when it nourishes the moral life of the nation for the sake of peace in the world (see www.pcusa. org/peacemaking/believers.pdf).

A reconciling vision of love through nonviolence

Eight years later, the Assembly stated, "Though the Reformed tradition has justified the resort to violence in response to particular forms of oppression, its emphasis on the reconciling vision of love presumes that the choice of nonviolence is more appropriate. As a way of life…it seeks peacefully to affirm creation, to respect the value and dignity of all human beings, and to recognize the potential for human fulfillment in all of God's people."

Richard Schlobohm

Security through justice

In 1994 the General Assembly advocated:

- The development of regional and global institutions that transcend the divisiveness of national structures and are capable of coping with global problems of war, peace, and conflict resolution, and that can address economic, social, and environmental problems that cut across nation-state boundaries in an interdependent world.
- The development of a new meaning of security based on common interest, cooperation, and trust, understanding that if any country is to be secure, all must be secure, and understanding that military power can never be the ultimate basis for world security.

The invasion of Iraq

In 2004: From the beginning, it was the judgment of many church leaders, both in the United States and elsewhere, that an invasion of Iraq would be unwise, immoral, and illegal. The 216th General Assembly concurred with this judgment (see www.pcusa. org/acswp/pdf/iraq-resolution.pdf).

The war in Afghanistan

In 2010, the Presbyterian News Service reported on the denomination's most recent action regarding Afghanistan: "The Presbyterian Church (U.S.A.)'s 219th General Assembly has called for the United States to end direct combat operations in Afghanistan, the denomination's first such statement since the war began in 2001. The action also asks the US government to

A Church Mandate for Palestine and Israel

At the meeting of the PC(USA) 218th General Assembly in 2008, a resolution was passed entitled "On Peace and Justice in Palestine and Israel." In the resolution, the church:

- Affirms the obligation of the church to speak to the governments of the United States and all other nations where it sees those governments violating the commandments of God;

- Endorses the "Amman Call" including its affirmation of the UN resolutions that are the basis of a projected "two-state" solution, a shared Jerusalem, and the human rights of refugees and occupied peoples;

- Commends the nonviolent witness of the Christians in Palestine and Israel;

- Encourages Presbyterian individuals, congregations, and councils to take pilgrimages and trips to Israel and Palestine that are in harmony with our principles [and that provide] opportunities to meet Israeli and Palestinian peacemakers and to engage in interfaith discussion of a range of perspectives.

(Read full text of Resolution 11-01 at https://www.pc-biz.org/IOBView. aspx?m=ro&id=507)

increase humanitarian and economic development assistance (and) calls for the United States to work with the Afghan people to facilitate peacemaking through consensus-building, open communication, economic incentives, and diplomacy."

God's call to peacemaking is absolute. God is not a god of destruction, abandonment or death, but of life, peace, and joy, who is jealous for a dynamic and full response from Christians who are called to be peacemakers in a warring world.

—*Peacemaking: The Believers' Calling* (p. 17), based on Hebrews 13:20, Ephesians 2:14-17

Part One: Perspective

> "I have spent a great deal of my life during the past 35 years advocating the rights of the Palestinian people to national self-determination, but I have always tried to do that with full attention paid to the reality of the Jewish people and what they suffered by way of persecution and genocide. The paramount thing is that the struggle for equality in Palestine/Israel should be directed toward a humane goal, that is, co-existence, and not further suppression and denial.
>
> —Edward Said, "Worldly Humanism v. the Empire-builders," *CounterPunch* August 4, 2003

Only a stone wall remains, marking the site of the Palestinian village Khirbat al-Duhayriyya in Khirbat district northeast of Al-Ramla. The village was attacked on July 10, 1948, by the Givati Brigade as part of Operation Dani. Israeli historian Benny Morris notes that the expulsion of the Palestinian residents of the Lydda-Ramla region in 1948 accounted for a full one-tenth of the Arab exodus from Palestine.

Noga Kadman

Six decades after the establishment of the state of Israel, there is growing awareness of the impact of that event on the Palestinian people. Broad recognition of the tragic history of Jewish persecution culminating in the Holocaust has been followed, if belatedly, by recognition of the price paid by the Palestinian people for European anti-semitism and Hitler's genocidal policies.

Even now, however, Americans are broadly familiar with the dominant Jewish narrative about Israel, but relatively few fully comprehend the Palestinian historical narrative and the ongoing story of their ethnic cleansing. This widespread imbalance in understanding is, itself, a barrier to peace. In his book *The Ethnic Cleansing of Palestine*, Israeli historian Ilan Pappe observes that retrieving the Palestinian story is "the very first step we must take if we ever want reconciliation to have a chance, and peace to take root, in the torn lands of Palestine and Israel."

Those who genuinely support the rights of both Arabs and Jews in the Middle East to live in peace must recognize the interdependence of the two peoples in their pursuit of human rights, security, and peaceful coexistence as equals. It does not diminish the importance of the Jewish narrative about Israel to advocate an equivalent awareness of the Palestinian experience both past and present.

A Jewish narrative: evolving attitudes

BY MARK BRAVERMAN

ZIONISM WAS the answer to the anti-Semitism of Christian Europe. The failure, despite the Enlightenment, to establish Jews as an emancipated, accepted group in Europe in the 18th and 19th centuries and the rise of political anti-Semitism in the late 19th century gave birth to political Zionism under the leadership of Theodore Herzl.

Zionism expressed the powerful drive of the Jewish people to establish themselves as a nation among other nations with a land of their own in which to achieve self-determination. The story of Jewish survival despite constant persecution at the hands of their oppressors is deeply embedded in the cultural DNA of the Jewish people.

Modern political Zionism springs from the Jewish experience over two thousand years of Jewish history; this experience colors the culture and the policies of the modern state of Israel. Although Zionism was a secular ideology, a religious version flourished after statehood, in which this reclamation of power was linked to a messianically-tinged belief in the fulfillment of God's promise to Abraham in the Biblical covenant.

In the dominant Jewish narrative about the birth of the State of Israel—a story until recently almost universally accepted throughout the Western world—the story of Israel's birth recapitulates Jewish history. In this story, the armies of the Jews' enemies had massed to destroy them time and again throughout history. But the founding of Israel changed history: the Jewish people fought back, defended themselves, prevented the disaster, and triumphed over their foes.

The Nazi Holocaust plays a dominant role in modern Israeli culture. The State of Israel is proof that in spite of the most extreme and systematic effort to destroy the Jewish people, they survived. Though this formulation of the relationship between the Nazi Holocaust and Zionism is commonplace, the historical reality is more complicated.

The stunning Israeli victory in the 1967 "Six-Day War," in which Israel conquered the Sinai, the West Bank, and Syria's Golan Heights, created a sense of euphoria in Israel and

Above left: "The Jews Who Will It Will Have Their State" (Zeev Raban, 1947) Theodore Herzl, after witnessing French mobs shouting "Death to the Jews" during the Dreyfus Affair, resolved that there was only one solution to Europe's persistent anti-Semitism: the mass migration of Jews to a land that they could call their own. Within a few years, Herzl had inaugurated the Zionist project with the goal of establishing a Jewish state in Palestine.

Above center and right: Zionist literature and graphic art, pre- and post-statehood, promoted images of tan, athletic men and women. The Jew, for millennia seen as servile, helpless, and excluded from the power structure, is now strong, self-determined, no longer a victim, and tied heroically to the land.

throughout the Jewish world. Israel's ambassador to the UN, Abba Eban, delivered a stirring address at the conclusion of that conflict, emphasizing and reinforcing the image of the tiny, beleaguered David of Israel vanquishing the Goliath of the armies of five Arab nations arrayed against it. The Biblical and messianic overtones of Israel's victory became predominant in Israeli culture. This feeling is seen as driving the activity to settle the occupied territories with Jewish Israelis, a process that has accelerated throughout the 60-plus years since 1948.

The power and persistence of the dominant Jewish narrative has had and continues to exert a powerful influence in the political sphere. A prime example is the belief that Israel has no partner for peace. Many, if not most, Israelis as well as diaspora Jews believe that there is "no choice" but to fight—that talking, sharing, and compromise will lead to disaster. The episodic outbreak of violence on the part of Palestinians and the growth of Palestinian political parties that accept violence as a legitimate form of resistance to occupation has lent support to that belief. Many Jews hold the

Safe haven: ingathering of the exiles

Immediately upon establishing the state in 1948, Israel opened its borders to Jewish refugees from around the world. Holocaust survivors streamed in from displaced persons camps from across Europe. Israel's stated purpose is to provide a haven for Jews to live in security and to be a center for the development of a vibrant Jewish culture.

> We [Israelis] do not distinguish between levels of hostility nor do we view our enemies as rivals with possibly legitimate needs; they are all against us all the time, and all we can do is defend ourselves.

—Avraham Burg, former speaker of the Israeli Knesset and author, *The Holocaust is Over; We Must Rise from Its Ashes*

view expressed in this often-repeated statement: "If the Arabs were to put down their arms, there would be peace in a minute. If Israel were to lay down its arms, there would be a bloodbath, a second Holocaust."

IN AMERICA TODAY there is a range of Jewish attitudes toward Israel. The first is the "pragmatic" approach, which can also be called the appeal to "enlightened self-interest." "The Occupation," so this position goes, "is bad for Israel. Denying self-determination for Palestinians and subjecting them to the humiliation of a military administration breeds hatred and desperation, which is then visited upon Israelis in the form of violence."

Some American Jewish organizations who are opposed to the occupation but concerned that by voicing these concerns they will be labeled "Pro-Palestinian" adopt this position. "Israel," they say, "should smarten up and change its policies if it wants to live in peace and limit the economic drain of unending conflict." In informal conversations with some Jewish Americans who articulate this position, they may confess that

their position is really more strongly negative about Israeli policy, but that they feel it important to hew to this line for strategic purposes, in order to maintain credibility with the Jewish establishment as well as with government legislators in today's "pro-Israel" climate in the US.

Some Jewish progressives are more willing to speak directly to human rights and justice issues, while still holding on to a Zionist position. These voices acknowledge the issue of justice, but attempt to do this within the context of Jewish mainstream assumptions of entitlement with respect to the rights of the Jews to historic Palestine. This viewpoint limits the discourse to "the Occupation" and Israeli actions since1967. It minimizes, avoids, or even denies the now well-documented history of the expulsion of three quarters of a million Palestinians from their cities and villages between 1947 and 1949.

Jewish critics of this position point out that avoiding the issue of the dispossession of the Palestinians fails to validate the experience of the other and maintains a position of Jewish ascendancy. Finally, it avoids the fundamental question, which is how a Jewish State, founded as a haven and a homeland for Jews, can provide justice and fair treatment for its non-Jewish citizenry. It avoids the related

and equally fundamental question of demography—the issue that, above all others, drives Israeli foreign policy and fuels the current political and military conflict.

On the whole, Jews outside of Israel across a wide spectrum from "establishment" to "progressive" until recently have preferred to keep

Dr. Mark Braverman, a clinical psychologist and organizational consultant, is executive director of holylandpeace.org and serves on the advisory board of Friends of Sabeel North America. He is the author of *Fatal Embrace: Christians, Jews and the Search for Peace in the Holy Land.* Since 2006 he has devoted his full-time attention to Israel-Palestine peacemaking.

these questions off limits. Increasingly, however, Jews inside and outside of Israel have begun to ask how Israel can become the true democracy it proclaims itself to be in its Declaration of Independence—a country for all its citizens. What, these Jews are asking, can it mean to be truly "pro-Israel?" What would it mean to have an Israel committed, not to higher walls, but to opening Israel's vibrant culture to cooperation and exchange with the Arab world in which it lives? Indeed, Israelis and Jews around the world, along with Christians who want the best for the Jewish people, are seeing that the future for Israel lies in its opening itself up to coexistence with the Palestinian people with whom it shares the land, rather than further isolating itself behind walls of concrete and military power.

Jewish activists in San Francisco (above) and Seattle (right) are part of a fast-growing movement among American Jews who are asking important questions about what it means to be "pro-Israel." In the process, these Jews are challenging the mainstream establishment institutions that claim to speak for the entire community.

The past two decades have seen steady growth in support for Jewish organizations that challenge the dominant mainstream narrative on Zionism and Israel. Recognizing that the two peoples are destined to share the land, many Jews recognize that the aspirations of Palestinians and Israelis are inextricably linked and that Jewish life in Israel/Palestine cannot flourish without respecting the human rights of Palestinians.

Joanna Kent Katz

A Palestinian narrative: then and now

BY NADIA HIJAB

WHEN ASKED TO describe what their cause is all about, most Palestinians will begin with the Balfour Declaration of November 2, 1917, when Britain promised the still small Zionist movement a "national home" in Palestine. Some will go farther back to 1897 and the Basel conference, where Zionism was born.

Palestinians start in the past because they have lived the history of their dispossession every day since 1917. And they can never forget the original sin, the flagrant injustice of an imperial power promising their country to another people. The Palestinians always ask: Why should we pay for what the Europeans did to the Jews? In 1917 the number of Arabs in Palestine—Muslims, Christians, and Jews—was about 650,000. A few thousand Zionist Jews had emigrated to Palestine since the end of the 19th century.

The Palestinians resisted British rule and plans for their country. They have always seen Israel as both a result and a continuation of 19th century colonialism. And, indeed, Israel's colonization continues to this day through the settlements it is building in the Palestinian territories occupied in 1967.

My mother's family left their home and their lands on April 28, 1948, seeking shelter in Syria from the clashes in Palestine and planning to return when quiet was restored. A few days earlier, on April 9, two terrorist Jewish groups (whose leaders both later became Israeli prime ministers) had massacred Palestinians at Deir Yassin and a Zionist whispering campaign

A Palestinian Arab family gathers hastily-packed boxes, bundles, chickens, and ducks on the dock in Haifa, Palestine, April 1948. Thousands of Palestinians from Haifa fled the advancing Zionist army and were evacuated on British military ships. As refugees, they believed they were leaving their lives, homes, and possessions temporarily; they were never permitted to return, and what they left behind was appropriated by Zionist statebuilders.

LIFE Magazine | palestineremembered.com

urged Palestinians to flee, to "remember Deir Yassin." My grandmother, a widow, had eight children; she and her four grown children got jobs to sustain the younger ones.

As a result of the creation of Israel in 1948, over 750,000 Palestinians fled or were forced to flee. They were never allowed back to their land and homes, in violation of international law. Palestinians struggled to survive their dispossession. The majority hailed from farms and villages and lived in refugee camps in Jordan, Lebanon, Syria, and Egypt, where millions live to this day. The ones with education found work and re-settled in Arab countries and around the world.

Richard Schlobohm

Nadia Hijab is a senior fellow at the Institute for Palestine Studies, an author, and a development consultant to international organizations. She co-founded the US Campaign to End the Israeli Occupation and serves on its advisory board.

The Palestinians who stayed on their land began the life of Arabs in a Jewish state. Although they were granted citizenship, they lived under Israeli military orders between 1949 and 1966—including curfews, detentions, and expulsions. The 1.5 million Palestinians now in Israel experience inequality and discrimination.

It is sometimes hard for people to understand the Palestinian attachment to their homes and their land. It is partly because this was an agricultural society rooted in the soil. But it is also because our society and country are so much part of how we Palestinians define ourselves. Being homeless means being rootless, living without a sense of belonging, always exposed to threat.

Perhaps the hardest part of the Palestinian struggle was to counter the myths the Zionist movement had spread to justify taking the land. One

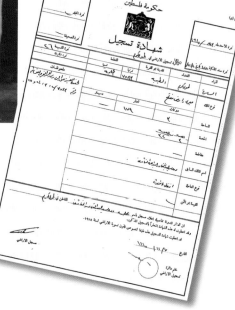

In pre-1948 Palestine, the Nashif family earned a comfortable livelihood from agriculture and shopkeeping. The author's grandmother carried all the family's land deeds with her when she left Palestine, taking the box with her from country to country—but she died without ever going back home. The deed below shows family ownership of land around the village (now town) of Taybeh; the family also lost land between Taybeh and the Mediterranean Sea in 1948.

Above: The author's grandparents with their first five children; three more would follow by 1945. The author's mother, Abla, is at far right. The Nashif family fled Palestine in 1948, settling as exiles in Syria; from there, descendants have become part of the Palestinian global diaspora.

such myth was a "land without a people for a people without a land." But Palestine was settled and had been for millennia one of the oldest continuously inhabited parts of the world.

Another Zionist myth was "making the desert bloom." In reality, the Palestinians were such good farmers of the country known in Biblical times as "the land of milk and honey" that in the late 1800s a US consul wrote back home and said Florida orange producers could learn from the Palestinian farmers' techniques.

Even though the Palestinians have dreamed of turning the clock back to 1917, the earliest PLO political programs recognized that the Jewish community in Palestine was there to stay. In the 1960s, the PLO advocated a secular, democratic state in all of Palestine for Muslims, Christians, and Jews.

> My grandmother always said the Palestinians never had a problem with the Jews as people. When her father would take her with him from Taybeh to Jaffa on one of his trips to market their produce, "We would share a meal with a Jewish family and spend the night with a Christian family."

The second PLO program, developed by 1974, was for two states living side by side, Israel constituting 78% of the country and Palestine the remaining 22% (lands occupied by Israel in the 1967 war). This has since been the basis of many peace plans—none implemented.

PALESTINIANS NO LONGER believe that Israel wants peace or that it will recognize that they have rights in Palestine. If Israel does want peace, then why has the number of Israeli settlers doubled since 1993 to some 527,000 today?

Israel always expresses fears about its security, but how does the colonization of Palestinian land contribute to Israel's security? On the contrary, the violence of the occupation, the endless injustice, and the hopelessness of life without rights have escalated the violence. The first suicide bombing against Israel took place in 1994, after 27 years of Israeli occupation.

Besides, Israel is one of the strongest states in the world, in military terms, and is a nuclear power believed to have between 200 and 400 warheads.

Oppressed people will always resist injustice. Most Palestinian resistance is nonviolent, but that fact rarely makes it into the American media. The first Palestinian uprising against the Israeli occupation in late 1987 was an almost completely nonviolent movement by civil society.

More recently, given the failure of the peace process and the weakness of the PLO, Palestinian civil society has taken the lead in advancing nonviolent strategies to bring an end to Israel's occupation. All who believe in justice are called to support boycott, divestment, and sanctions (BDS) against Israel until it upholds international law.

For Palestinians, a major source of hope is that many Jews, in Israel and around the world, are active in campaigning for Palestinian human rights. The involvement of Jews is an important expression of solidarity that greatly contributes to future peace among Palestinians and Jews.

Remembering the Nakba

The United Nations answered the Palestinian refugee crisis in 1948 by establishing tent camps in Jordan, Syria, Lebanon, and the Palestinian areas controlled by Egypt (Gaza) and Jordan (the West Bank). Those camps, now densely packed concrete slums, have been home to registered refugees for more than 60 years. Today, the Palestinians displaced in 1948 and subsequent wars and their descendants number over seven million.

> It must be clear that there is no room for both peoples in this country…. this will not bring about the State of Israel….and there is no way besides transferring the Arabs from here to neighboring countries.

—Joseph Weitz, director of the Jewish National Land Fund, 1940, from *My Diary and Letters to the Children*, vol. II

O N MAY 15, 1948, the British Mandate of Palestine ended, and Israel became an independent state. Contrary to Israeli versions of the story, Palestinians did not voluntarily abandon their homes. 250,000 already had been forcibly removed by Jewish militias before that date; 500,000 more were evicted by the Israeli military between May 15, 1948, and the Armistice of February 12, 1949.†

The United Nations adopted a plan to partition Palestine (Resolution 181) on November 29, 1947, in spite of the vigorous objections of Palestinian leaders and the Arab world. The partition plan allocated to Israel 54% of Mandate Palestine (containing over 400 Palestinian villages within its borders), although the Jewish population owned only 6% of the land at the time. Resolution 181 included no mechanism to keep the peace or prevent ethnic cleansing. Predictably, the indigenous Palestinians rejected any division of the land on which they had lived and farmed for centuries, particularly a division as inequitable as the one proposed. Palestinians protested with riots and looting, and Jewish forces retaliated. Ethnic cleansing began in December 1947 while British soldiers stood by and watched.

On March 10, 1948, (well before surrounding Arab nations joined the conflict), David Ben Gurion (who later became Israel's first prime minister) and his advisors implemented Plan Dalet, a military operation to depopulate and destroy Palestinian villages. The goal was the ethnic cleansing of Palestine's non-Jewish population. That night orders were sent to militia units providing detailed methods of destruction and listing the villages and urban neighborhoods to be "cleansed." In the months surrounding Israel's creation, Zionist forces committed at least 30 intentional massacres, killing thousands of unarmed Palestinians; 531 villages were destroyed; eleven urban neighborhoods were emptied of their inhabitants.

Mordechai Maklef (who later became the Israeli army Chief of Staff) ordered the Carmeli Brigade in Haifa to "kill any Arab you encounter; torch all inflammable objects and force doors open with explosives." Israeli historian Ilan Pappe describes the resulting exodus of Palestinians in his book *The*

Ethnic Cleansing of Palestine: over 85,000 Palestinians living in Haifa and Jaffa were forced to exit their cities through the local seaports. Some tried to escape on small fishing boats while the Zionist militia attacked with rockets and guns. Overcrowded with their living cargo, many boats turned over and sank with all their passengers.

Six decades later, refugees await return, restitution

During the war in 1948, Zionist planners took measures to prevent Palestinians from returning to the homes they had left to escape the conflict. In August 1948 a "Transfer Committee" was charged with the destruction of depopulated Palestinian villages or their repopulation with Jewish immigrants newly arrived in Palestine. The Absentee Law, passed in December 1948, legalized the confiscation of vacant Palestinian properties. Prevented from returning home, some displaced Palestinians settled elsewhere in Palestine. Most were forced out of the

Kafr Bir'im, located in the northern Galilee near the Lebanon border, was captured on October 31, 1948, by the Haganah (Israeli militia that became the Israeli Defense Forces) during Operation Hiram (inset photo). Most of the inhabitants were evacuated by the Israeli army to a nearby town. Archbishop Elias Chacour's autobiography recounts how the Israeli army rounded up the men and older boys in the village in the spring of 1949 and trucked them to the border with Jordan. The soldiers ordered them to cross the border, Chacour writes, then opened fire, aiming just above their heads. On September 16, 1953, a joint Israeli army-air force operation bombed the now-empty village, destroying all its buildings except the village church and school. At the same time, 290 acres of land belonging to the village were expropriated by the state. The story of the village is documented in a 2007 film titled *The Presence of Absence in the Ruins of Kafr Bir'im*.

†Source: UNRWA

Zionism and ethnic cleansing: voices of Israeli leaders

"The Arabs will have to go, but one needs an opportune moment for making it happen, such as a war."

—David Ben-Gurion, Israel's founding father and first prime minister, 1937

"Neither Jewish ethics nor Jewish tradition can disqualify terrorism as a means of combat....First and foremost, terrorism is for us a part of the political battle...."

—Yitzhak Shamir, seventh prime minister, 1943

"Eretz Israel, [the 'Land of Israel,' including the West Bank and Gaza] will be restored to the people of Israel. All of it. And forever."

—Menachem Begin, sixth prime minister, 1954

"[Israel must] invent dangers, and to do this it must adopt the method of provocation-and-revenge...And above all—let us hope for a new war with the Arab countries, so that we may finally get rid of our troubles and acquire our space...."

—Moshe Sharett, second prime minister, before the 1967 War

"It is the duty of Israeli leaders to explain to public opinion clearly and courageously...[that] there is no Zionism, colonialization [sic], or Jewish State without the eviction of the Arabs and the expropriation of their lands."

—Ariel Sharon, Minister of Defense, then prime minister, 1998

" The ideology that enabled the depopulation of half of Palestine's native people in 1948 is still alive and continues to drive the inexorable, sometimes indiscernible, cleansing of those Palestinians who live there today.

—Israeli historian Ilan Pappe, 2006

Large numbers of the refugees ended up in the Gaza Strip. Approximately 80% of the 1.6 million people in Gaza, or about 1.28 million people, are refugees and their descendants.

WITHIN ISRAEL'S borders, Palestinians face a different set of challenges as a result of their minority status in a self-defined Jewish state. Of the nearly one million Palestinians uprooted from their homes in 1948, some 150,000 remained within the boundaries of Israel. That population has grown to nearly 1.5 million. Some live in borders of the newly-formed Jewish state altogether. Predictably, refugees attempted to return to their former homes; Israel treated them as criminal infiltrators.

UN Security Council Resolution 194 (December 11, 1948) stated that "refugees wishing to return to their homes should be permitted to do so at the earliest practicable date and that those choosing not to return should be compensated for their property." Israel's admission to the United Nations was conditioned on its compliance with this resolution. In the decades since, numerous resolutions have called for the return of Palestinain refugees and the end of Israel's occupation of the West Bank and Gaza. Israel has not complied: while using Resolutions 181 and 194 as legal support for its creation, Israel has rejected other resolutions as non-binding.

There is a growing campaign to deny the legal rights of Palestinians as a *quid pro quo* for losses experienced by Jewish refugees to Israel from Arab countries after 1948. Palestinian exiles, naturally, see it as yet another injustice that their legal rights would be canceled out by Middle Eastern Jews' property claims. Furthermore, Israel has actively promoted and subsidized Jewish emigration from Middle Eastern countries in its chronic struggle to build and maintain a Jewish majority.

Palestinian villages depopulated in 1948 and razed by Israel

Haifa · Sea of Galilee · Nazareth · Mediterranean Sea · Nablus · WEST BANK · Tel Aviv Jaffa · Jerusalem · Gaza · GAZA STRIP · Hebron · Dead Sea · Beersheba

531 Palestinian villages were emptied and razed by Israel as a result of the 1948 conflict. Some of these villages' former inhabitants and their descendants have become part of the Palestinian diaspora. Others live within Israel today and experience discrimination as non-Jews living in a Jewish state.

The ongoing Nakba: Hebron

In April 1968, less than a year after Israel's success in the Six-Day War, a few Israelis led by Rabbi Moshe Levinger rented a hotel room in the West Bank city of Hebron, ostensibly to celebrate Passover, then refused to leave, declaring their intention to create a permanent Jewish settlement there. Levinger's followers were spearheading a movement to settle Judea and Samaria, land they believed God had allotted to the Jews in the book of Deuteronomy.

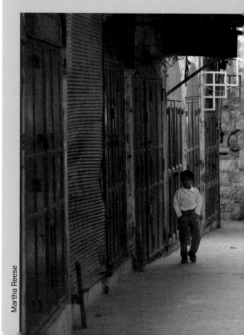

Martha Reese

rights as all other political states—no more, no less. As a theological matter, this makes God a party to Israel's breach of international law and abuse of human rights in the occupied territories. As a 2008 conference of the World Council of Churches on "The Promised Land" stated, "[T]he Bible must not be utilized to justify oppression…."

Over the past 63 years, since the birth of the modern state of Israel, the PC(USA) has supported the existence of Israel as a sovereign state within secure, internationally recognized borders, as well as the need for a neighboring, independent, sovereign Palestinian state. But it has never justified either state on theological or biblical grounds.† Theological claims to the land turn the conflict into a holy war by sacralizing it and removing all constraints on the use of violence. (The War on Gaza described on page 29 demonstrates official rejection of restraint.) Theological land claims have no standing in international law and stand in the way of peacemaking. And millennia of experience have proved that cosmic holy wars are not winnable.

Christian theology: the Covenant and the Promised Land

Christian tradition provides at least three reasons to reject the state of Israel's claim to land based on biblical texts.

First, the tragic consequences which often come about when ancient religious texts are removed from their historical context and used to justify contemporary political ideologies and programs. The human suffering and human rights violations produced by the long and seemingly intractable conflict between the modern state of Israel and the Palestinian people are a case in point and have stirred the Christian conscience world wide.

Second, the biblical requirement of obedience to God's way of justice and righteousness includes treating the stranger with kindness and hospitality, indeed as fellow citizens (Deuteronomy 10:12-22).

Third, the New Testament teaching that Christians are part of the Covenant through God's son, Jesus, whose call is to reconcile all people, Jew and Gentile, into a peaceable realm in which stewardship of the land is required of all and the ethic of love of neighbor is the basis of "kingdom" citizenship (Romans 11:17; 14:17-18; Matthew 22:37-40).

The genealogical claim to land

The founding narrative of the State of Israel links the modern-day Jews' claim to the land of Israel/Palestine to their direct genealogical descent from the ancient Israelites. Recent anthropological scholarship shows that this widespread belief is very likely a myth, not historical fact. Shlomo Sand is an expert on European history at the University of Tel Aviv, and author of the much-debated book *The Invention of the Jewish People*. (When first published, this book was on the best- seller list in Israel for 19 weeks.) Sand posits that the Jews were never exiled *en masse* from the Holy Land after the fall of The Temple in 70 CE, and that many European Jewish populations converted to the faith centuries later. Thus, he argues, many of today's Israelis who emigrated from Europe after World War II have little or no genealogical connection to the ancient land of Israel. Sand argues that the Palestinians of today are more likely the actual Semitic people who are descendents of the Jews of the time of Jesus. The attack on his research and his book have of course made him a controversial historian. In any case, the genealogical connection is not uniformly supported,

even within Israeli scholarship.

The genealogical picture is further complicated by the commonsense assumption among historians that some of today's Palestinians are descended from Jews who converted to Christianity or Islam. ††

Clearly, neither racial/ethnic nor biblical/theological claims to real estate in the Holy Land can bring peace and reconciliation. In the 21st century, we are left only with UN resolutions, international law, and universal human rights as the basis for a just resolution to this conflict.

Christian Zionism's flawed theology

Christian Zionism is a predominantly American movement that believes the modern state of Israel is the catalyst for the end of times, the fulfillment of biblical prophecy, and the return of Jesus with final judgment.

Bethlehem's inhabitants today are isolated and oppressed, surrounded by a 25-foot high concrete wall constructed by Israel. Jewish settlements are expanding on expropriated Palestinian land surrounding the city. Despite these dismal developments in the city of Christ's birth, there has been little outcry from concerned Christians around the world.

David Young

---

† See the 1987 PC(USA) study paper entitled "A Theological Understanding of the Relationship between Christians and Jews."

†† Shlomo Sand, *The Invention of the Jewish People*, pp. 179, 181, 186 [citing Ben Zion Dinur, *Israel in Exile, vol. 1* (1969); David Ben-Gurion and Yitzhak Ben-Zvi, *Eretz Israel in the Past and the Present* (1979), p. 122.].

Christian Zionism has become a significant political force in the United States. In an October 12, 2002, appearance on *60 Minutes*, televangelist Jerry Falwell said: "I think we can count on President Bush to do the right thing for Israel every time."

Televangelist John Hagee has recently developed a lobbying organization, Christians United for Israel (CUFI), which is well on its way to achieving its stated goal of having Christian Zionist offices and networks in every state of the union. CUFI fully supports the work of the American Israel Public Affairs Committee (AIPAC), the powerful pro-Israel lobbying organization.

CHRISTIAN ZIONISM is now, according to public polls, part of the American social/religious fabric with 59% of Americans believing the rapture will be an historical event (Gallup, 1999); 66% expecting Jesus' imminent return (National Opinion, 1996); and 46% believing that the state of Israel is the fulfillment of Biblical prophecy (National Opinion, 1996).

Hagee and other Christian Zionist leaders and organizations oppose the internationally accepted formula for a

Core beliefs of Christian Zionism

The Covenant

God's covenant with Israel is eternal and unconditional; the promises of land given to Abraham will never be overturned. The church has not replaced Israel; therefore, Israel's privileges have never been revoked.

The Church

God's plan has always been for the redemption of Israel. When Israel failed to follow Jesus, the church was born as an afterthought or "parenthesis." At the rapture the church will be removed, and Israel will once again become God's primary agent in the world. We now live in "the times of the Gentiles," which will conclude soon. There are two covenants now at work, that given through Moses and the covenant of Christ. The new covenant in no way makes the older covenant obsolete.

Blessing modern Israel

Genesis 12:3 is applied literally and is applied to modern Israel: "I will bless those who bless you, and the one who curses you I will curse." Christians have a spiritual obligation to bless Israel and "pray for the peace of Jerusalem." While many Christians throughout history have also believed it important to observe the injunction of Genesis 12:3 in regard to the Jews, Christian Zionism links this specifically to support of the modern state of Israel. To fail to support Israel's political survival as a Jewish state will incur divine judgment.

Prophecy

The prophetic books of the Bible specifically refer to events today, though some may also refer to events in biblical times. Looking at Daniel 7, for instance, if we possess the right interpretative skills, we can see current events foreshadowed in it. This quest for prophecy has spawned countless books of end-time speculation (i.e., *The Late Great Planet Earth*, the *Left Behind* series, etc.) involving the state of Israel based on biblical prophecy.

Modern Israel and eschatology

The modern state of Israel is a catalyst for the prophetic end-time countdown. If these are the last days, then we should expect an unraveling of civilization, the rise of evil, the loss of international peace and equilibrium, a coming antichrist, and tests of faithfulness to Israel. Above all, political alignments today will determine our position on the fateful day of Armageddon. Since the crisis of 9/11 and the wars in Afghanistan and Iraq, it has been easy to persuade a large segment of the public that history is unraveling precisely as dispensationalism predicted.

All these beliefs are rejected by the historic mainline Christian tradition.

just peace between Israel and the Palestinians based on an independent and sovereign state of Israel alongside an independent, sovereign, and contiguous Palestinian state.

Christian Zionism elevates the rights of Israeli Jews while denying human and civil rights to Palestinians. It encourages Israeli policies that seek to drive Palestinians from their homeland and expand illegal Jewish settlements, and it supports the use of military force rather than diplomacy for resolving political differences between Israelis and Palestinians.

Christian Zionism distorts Christian theology by omitting Jesus' command to love our enemies and seek peace based on justice.

Some Jews recognize the threat posed by Christian Zionism's brand of allegiance to Israel. Israeli journalist Gershom Gorenberg, in a *60 Minutes* interview on October 12, 2002, warns that "Christian Zionists do not see Jews as real people but as actors in their religious drama, where two-thirds of Jews are killed in one act, and the remainder must convert to Christianity."

John Hagee, televangelist and founder of Christians United for Israel, opposes any withdrawal by Israel from occupied territory. Addressing an AIPAC conference in March 2007, Hagee expressed concern that "in the coming months yet another attempt will be made to parcel out parts of Israel in a futile effort to appease Israel's enemies in the Middle East." But Hagee is confident in the power of his followers to shape the course of history. "The sleeping giant of Christian Zionism has awakened," he boasts. "There are 50 million Christians standing up and applauding the State of Israel."

The American conversation

OST AMERICANS are fairly familiar with the dominant Jewish narrative about Israel, but relatively few know the Palestinian narrative and the ongoing story of their ethnic cleansing. One reason for this is the cultural familiarity with scriptures common to Judaism and Christianity. Another is the presence in the United States of a well-assimilated Jewish community that has built institutions with a capacity to engage with public opinion—and the relative weakness of Palestinian advocacy institutions.

Skewed media coverage creates distorted perceptions

Another important factor in shaping public understanding is media coverage which has, historically, presented a skewed representation of the conflict. Bias in print and broadcast media typically manifests itself in several ways: word choice, e.g., the use of the term "by-pass roads" instead of "segregated roads"; placement, e.g., giving front-page coverage to Israel and burying a story about Palestine on the back page; lack of verification, e.g., accepting government "spin" as truth; selective reporting, as in maximal coverage of Israeli victims of Palestinian violence and minimal reporting on the victims of Israeli violence; decontextualization, as in reporting Hamas rocket attacks on Israel but failing to report the repeated assassinations and military incursions by Israel that provoke such attacks; coercion or censorship, like Israel's frequent denial of media access to the occupied territories and the targeting of reporters and photojournalists by Israeli tanks and snipers.

The most frequent form of bias is omission. Rarely does the mainstream US media report the daily violence of settlers against Palestinians or the ongoing nonviolent demonstrations by Palestinians against the construc-

tion of the Wall and the confiscation of their land. Rare, too, are stories that describe the overall impact of the occupation on both Palestinians and Israelis (though such coverage does appear in the Israeli media).

If the US media is overly dependent on official Israeli spokespersons, they are relatively deaf to the voices of Palestinians.

US media are scrupulous about reporting the official Israeli version of events, which often describes acts of Israeli aggression as "responses" to Palestinian violence. Too seldom do media outlets include a Palestinian perspective on the Israeli actions that generate acts of Palestinian resistance, both violent and nonviolent.

Professors John Mearsheimer of the University of Chicago and Stephen Walt of Harvard University have published an analysis of the dynamics of what they call the "Israel Lobby" and its effects on public discourse in the US. "A key part of preserving positive public attitudes toward Israel is to ensure that the mainstream media's coverage of Israel and the Middle East consistently favors Israel and does not call US support into question in any way," they write in their book *The Israel Lobby and U.S. Foreign Policy* (p. 169). "[T]he American media's coverage of Israel tends to be strongly biased in Israel's favor, especially when compared with news coverage in other democracies." The chapter on "Dominating Public Discourse" describes the "objectionable tactics" used to create bias in the media, to promote one-sided analyses by think tanks, and to police the academic community.

Skewed coverage is no accident, writes Walter Rodgers, Jerusalem bureau chief for CNN from 1995 to 2000. "At the height of the second Palestinian intifada, Richard Griffiths, the editorial director of CNN, admonished me: 'You have to remember, Walt, there are two standards of reporting at CNN, one for Israel and the other for the rest of the world.' Like many in US news organizations responsible for Middle East coverage at that time, Griffiths had just taken a terrible beating from Jewish-American pressure groups as well as from his own avowedly pro-Israel management."[†]

Fortunately for those interested in peace, signs of change are on the horizon. Jewish Voice for Peace's Muzzlewatch Project is monitoring attempts to censor or slant media coverage and other forms of bias—a field that has, until recently, been dominated by multiple organizations monitoring the media for "anti-Israel" bias.

The changing tone of the debate

The last decade has produced groundbreaking writing that focuses on the key issues underlying the present situation. Much of this work takes direct aim at the myths, falsehoods, and denials that have been presented to the world at large and that help perpetuate the cycle of violence and political stalemate. Ilan Pappe, Avi Shlaim, and other Israeli "new historians" have published a side of the story that has, until recently, been absent from the public square. Increasingly, the American public is becoming aware that the obstacles to peace are complex and that Israel, far from being an innocent victim, bears major responsibility.

Former US President Jimmy Carter has reached many with his publication in late 2006 of a controversial book, *Palestine: Peace Not Apartheid*. In the book, he writes: "In order to perpetu-

† Walter Rodgers, *The Christian Century Magazine*, May 19, 2009, www.christiancentury.org/article.lasso?id=6941

ate the occupation, Israeli forces have deprived their unwilling subjects of basic human rights. No objective person could personally observe existing conditions in the West Bank and dispute these statements."

In published writing and speaking appearances, Archbishop Tutu of South Africa, who, like President Carter, compares Israel's policies in the occupied territories to South African apartheid, has called for a global social movement to oppose Israel's violation of human rights.

A GROWING CHORUS OF Israeli journalists and social critics expose the political and social damage inflicted on the state of Israel itself by the subjugation of Palestinians in the West Bank and Gaza; increasingly, Americans are listening to this important "other voice" on Israel.

In 2006 American-born Israeli historian Gershom Gorenberg published *The Accidental Empire: Israel and the Birth of the Settlements, 1967-1977*, showing how the power of the religious-settler movement and the failure of political will on the part of the Israeli government—including the "moderate" left-wing—has been responsible for continued conflict and the failure of successive peace initiatives. Avraham Burg, former speaker of the Israeli Knesset and former chairman of the Jewish Agency and World Zionist Organization, warns that Israel, "Holocaust-obsessed, militaristic, xenophobic, and, like Germany in the nineteen-thirties, vulnerable to an extremist minority," is in danger of losing its status as a democracy.

The internet has become an important alternative to corporate media for coverage of the conflict. Electronic Intifada is an influential, respected internet source of news and analysis from a Palestinian perspective.

Public awareness is also increasing

as the result of high-profile attempts to silence critics of Israel. Attacks on Jimmy Carter, Archbishop Desmond Tutu, and Professor Norman Finkelstein have exposed the tactics used to stifle open debate on US foreign policy in ways that myriad similar cases affecting lesser-known individuals have failed to do.

Jewish Voice for Peace, American Jews for a Just Peace, International Anti-Zionist Network and a number of other Jewish-led peace and justice organizations have been growing rapidly and gaining recognition over the past several years. The Washington, DC-based US Campaign to End the Occupation is a coalition of over 320 local, regional, and national groups that oppose the Israeli occupation, advocate the application of international law, and challenge US policy toward Israel-Palestine. In 2008, J Street, a new Jewish lobby in Washington, DC, was founded to counter the influence of the American Israel Public Affairs Committee (AIPAC) and "promote meaningful American leadership to end the Arab-Israeli and Palestinian-Israel conflicts peacefully and diplomatically." Also in 2008, the highly respected Israeli human rights monitoring organization B'Tselem

established an office in Washington, DC. Campus-based organizations such as Students for Justice in Palestine are proliferating on university campuses; Adalah–NY has implemented creative strategies including street theater for raising awareness.

Churches in the US are also showing an increasing willingness to challenge Israel's discrimination and dispossession of Palestinians. Disciples of Christ, Episcopalians, Lutherans, Methodists, Presbyterians, and the United Church of Christ are initiating educational, global mission, and advocacy projects, including initiatives to hold US companies accountable for their activities that contribute to and profit from Israel's military occupation of Palestine.

Many of those working to educate, inform, and mobilize are individuals who have traveled to Israel/Palestine for personal, direct experience with the conflict. Having heard from Palestinian and Israeli peacemakers challenging the status quo, these Americans return home with a powerful desire to share what they've learned. As more Americans are offered a balanced alternative to the Israel-centric perspective that has dominated during our lifetimes, it is to be hoped that there will be growing acceptance of the necessary conditions for a resolution of the conflict.

A burgeoning list of books challenging common assumptions about the history of the Israeli-Palestinian conflict and the impact of the US has helped readers gain a better grasp of reality than what is available from corporate media.

Part Two: Occupation

1946
- ■ Palestinian-owned land
- ▢ Jewish-owned land

1947 U.N. Plan
- ■ Land designated for a Palestinian state
- ▢ Land designated for a Jewish state

1949–1967
- ■ Palestinian land
- ▢ Jewish land (military and civil control)

2007
- ■ Palestinian land
- ▢ Jewish land (military and civil control)

Map: original version by NAD-PLO; adapted from Oren Medicks, 1999. Published in *Occupation Magazine*; modified by Engin Çoban.

Following its victory in the Six-Day War of 1967, the government of Israel was divided about what to do with the territories newly conquered in battle. Some, including some of the Israeli government's legal advisors, made clear that keeping these territories and incorporating them into the state of Israel would contravene international law and international agreements which they had signed. The strong preference of the ruling Likud party, however, was to maintain control of the conquered land and annex it incrementally.

Decades of peace initiatives have yielded only relentless, incremental loss for the Palestinian people. While generations of Palestinians have been subjected to ever-diminishing levels of education, health, prosperity, and hope, the peace process has served as a smokescreen for Israel's annexation and settlement of Palestinian land and the confinement of the Palestinian people into ever-shrinking zones of isolation and deprivation.

2009
- ▢ Limited Palestinian sovereignty
- ▲ Jewish settlements beyond the Green Line
- ▢ Israeli military and civil control

Jenin

Tulkarm

Nablus   ELON MOREH

Qalqilya

ARIEL   MA'ALE EFRAIM

SHILO

Ramallah   Jericho

GIVAT ZEEV

MA'ALE ADUMIM

Jerusalem

BETAR   Bethlehem

EFRAT

Hebron

SHIMA

Map: www.passia.org

EAST JERUSALEM HAS been militarily occupied territory since June 1967. The international community, including the United Nations and the United States, does not recognize the 1967 annexation of 70 sq. km of mostly vacant West Bank land to the municipal boundaries of West Jerusalem. The Geneva Convention prohibits unilateral annexation of territory acquired by military conquest.

On June 5, 1967, Israel initiated a preemptive strike by bombing and then invading Egypt, Jordan, and Syria with the goal of expanding the boundaries of the state. Six days later Israel controlled Gaza, Sinai, the Golan, and the West Bank along with both halves of Jerusalem. Almost at once the Israelis began reshaping the city by clearing a space along the western wall of the mosque compound known to Muslims as the Haram al Sharif and to Jews as the Temple Mount. This operation involved the demolition of the 135 dwellings that constituted the Magharibah (Moroccan) quarter, along with a waqf (religious foundation) founded in the 12th century. All were bulldozed in one afternoon. The 1,000 residents of the quarter were scattered into the streets "at a few minutes notice." Another 5,500 Palestinians were driven out of the Jewish quarter.

On June 27, 1967, the Knesset passed legislation extending Israeli laws to East Jerusalem, resulting in annexation. The Israeli government expanded the municipal area of West Jerusalem by more than 70 sq. km to 108 sq. km. Israeli leaders announced that the process of integration was "irreversible and not negotiable."

The boundaries of the newly expanded municipality were gerrymandered to exclude Arab population centers, many of which were historically considered Jerusalem suburbs, and to include as much empty land as possible, particularly if it was prime agricultural land. On July 14, 1967, the UN General Assembly passed resolution 2254(ES-V) calling on Israel to rescind all measures already taken and desist from any further action that would alter the status of Jerusalem. This and other resolutions were simply ignored, with the backing of the United States.

Palestinians present at the time of the census following the 1967 War were granted "permanent resident" status, the same status as foreign citizens who are temporarily living in Israel, although these Palestinians were born in Jerusalem and had no other home. Treating these Palestinians as foreigners who entered Israel

> "Many of [Israel's] current illegal actions in and around the city have limited security justifications....Israeli 'facts on the ground'—including new settlements, construction of the barrier, discriminatory housing policies, house demolitions, restrictive permit regime, and continued closure of Palestinian institutions—increase Jewish Israeli presence in East Jerusalem, weaken the Palestinian community in the city, impede Palestinian urban development, and separate East Jerusalem from the rest of the West Bank....
>
> —European Union Heads of Mission Report on East Jerusalem, December 15, 2008

East Jerusalem

Har Homa was established by Israel in 1997 on Jebel Ghneim, occupied territory east of the Green Line. At the time, the US vetoed two different UN Security Council resolutions that called on Israel to stop its construction. Although Secretary of State Condoleezza Rice expressed official disapproval of Israel's 2008 expansion of Har Homa, no punitive measures were suggested or imposed.

is astonishing, since it was Israel that entered East Jerusalem in 1967. These "permanent residents" can vote in municipal elections, but are not allowed to vote for Knesset candidates, in contrast to Jewish citizens who moved into East Jerusalem after 1967.

Palestinian residents of East Jerusalem pay taxes but receive few benefits. The municipality has failed to invest significantly in infrastructure and services (such as roads, sidewalks, and water and sewage systems) in Jerusalem's Palestinian neighborhoods.

In 2003 Israel enacted a law that prohibits Palestinian residents of East Jerusalem or Israel proper from living with their spouses if the spouse is from the occupied territories. Since permits to travel to and from the occupied territories are hard to get, this law destroys family life.

hree generations of the Siam family became home-ess in Silwan when their home was destroyed under sraeli decree. Between 1994 and 2010, almost ,000 houses were demolished in East Jerusalem lone. From June 1967 to June 2010, about 25,000 omes have been demolished in the occupied erritories.

While Palestinian communities in Jerusalem and environs are being choked and demolished, homes in Jewish-only settlements are being constructed, often on land expropriated from Palestinian owners. Large, high density settlement blocs visually dominate modern East Jerusalem.

Settlement construction has been continuous from 1967 to the present. By the end of 2001, 46,978 housing units had been built; not one of these was allocated for Palestinians, who constitute one-third of the city's population.

Between November 2007 when the Annapolis peace talks began and December 2010 when the Obama-initiated peace talks ceased, 5,900 new settlement housing units have been approved. There are now over half a million settlers in the occupied territories, including some 200,000 in East Jerusalem.

Numerous settlements ringing East Jerusalem (including Har Homa, Gilo, Ramat Eshkol, East Talpiot, French Hill, and Malcha), are situated so as to irreversibly "Judaize" Jerusalem by creating facts on the ground that break up the Palestinian contiguity in Jerusalem and the West Bank.

Still more Palestinian land has been expropriated for the construction of ring roads and separation barriers that enable Jewish Israelis to move freely among settlements while paralyzing Palestinian movement.

Some of the land on which the Jewish settlement Nof Zion stands is owned by Palestinian families of the Jabal Al Mukhaber area of East Jerusalem. In 2005 the Palestinian owners of these tracts submitted an appeal to the Israeli High Court to prevent the building of Nof Zion, but the court rejected their petition. Nof Zion (Zion View) is one of 34 illegal settlements in East Jerusalem and the surrounding West Bank.

> The Israeli government and private Jewish groups are working in concert to build a human cordon around Jerusalem's Old City and its disputed holy sites, moving Jewish residents into Arab neighborhoods to consolidate their grip on strategic locations....The Israeli government has sometimes violated its own laws and regulations to advance the encircling effort....
>
> —John Ward Anderson, *Israelis Act to Encircle East Jerusalem Enclaves in Arab Areas, Illegal Building Projects Seen Intended to Consolidate Control*, Washington Post, February 7, 2005

Settlements

ISRAELI SETTLEMENTS are colonies for inhabitation by Israeli Jews only, constructed in the Palestinian territories of East Jerusalem and the West Bank which Israel occupied after the Six-Day War in June 1967. The view among many Jewish Israelis in power at that time was that the Six-Day War had provided redemption for the Land of Israel (Eretz Israel).

Planning for the strategic placement of settlements in the West Bank began immediately after this war and has been an integral policy of each elected government since then. "There must not be the slightest doubt regarding our intention to hold the areas of Judea and Samaria for ever," wrote Mattiyahu Drobless, architect of one of the takeover plans. By locating settlements on prominent hills, Israel could control all the Palestinian aquifers while also dominating the horizon as a constant, intimidating reminder of the Israeli conquest.

Since 1967 Israel has seized more than 40 percent of West Bank lands,

The Bush legacy

Publicly, the administration of George W. Bush opposed Israeli settlement construction. The Road Map of 2003, initiated by the US and backed by other members of the "Quartet" (US, UN, EU, and Russia), called on Israel to halt all construction in the settlements, including their "natural growth." At no point, however, did Israel stop settlement construction and expansion, including construction that Israel itself deems "illegal." US Secretary of State Rice issued periodic protests, calling settlement construction "not helpful" and "a problem," but no punitive measures were proposed, much less taken, against Israel for its noncompliance.

Israeli Prime Minister Netanyahu rejects Obama administration bans on settlement expansion, citing secret "agreements" and private "understandings" between his predecessor Ehud Olmert and the Bush administration that construction in existing Jewish settlements could continue as a quid pro quo for Israel's pull-out from Gaza in 2005.

allocating them to settlements erected over the years. Now, nearly half a million Israelis live in the occupied territories: 327,800† in over 121 settlements and 100 outposts in the West Bank and 200,000† in settlements in and around East Jerusalem. Although the international community regards all these colonies as a breach of international law and UN resolutions, the Israeli government has authorized and subsidized the settlements and provides services to the outposts. US foreign assistance contributes to their construction and defense. Israeli Jews are provided financial incentives to participate in the colonization of Palestinian land.

Israeli settlement colonies are a major obstacle to peace because, in the words of President George Bush, "Swiss cheese isn't going to work when it comes to the outline of a state." The colonies and the infrastructure that links them to Israel imprison Palestinians into isolated enclaves, eviscerate the Palestinian

> *While negotiations have been going on for 15 years, hundreds of thousands of Jewish settlers have moved in to occupy the West Bank. Palestinians say they can't have a state with Israeli settlers all over it, which the settlers say is precisely the idea.*
>
> — Bob Simon, CBS's *60 Minutes*, January 25, 2009

This settlement, built on a hill near Nablus, shows both permanent housing and mobile caravans. Caravans are often the first phase of illegal settlement activity, followed by permanent housing, then roads and other infrastructure. From small, isolated beachheads, settlements typically encroach further onto surrounding land and grow in population. Settlers sometimes engage in harrassment and violence toward Palestinian landowners in the vicinity.

economy, and prevent the creation of a viable, contiguous, sovereign, and independent Palestinian state.

Many thousands of acres around settlements are closed to Palestinian entry. Settlers have placed physical obstructions far from the last houses of the settlement, patrol paths that they have built on Palestinian land, and expel Palestinians from this land. The state of Israel also contributes to this expropriation of Palestinian land by building by-pass roads and buffer zones to connect these settlement-colonies with Israel. These segregated roads are off-limits to Palestinians who are cut-off from their schools, hospitals, markets, and extended families and friends.

Every Israeli government since 1967, whether led by Labor, Likud, or Kadima, has supported the colonization of more and more Palestinian land. In spite of promises made during peace talks beginning with Oslo in 1993, Israel has continued to create new settlements and expand existing ones. "What we're seeing is a classic example where a diplomatic initiative has the effect of accelerating settlement construction," observed Gershom Gorenberg in June 2008.

† *Report on Israeli Settlement in the Occupied Territories*, Foundation for Middle East Peace, Jan-Feb 2011.

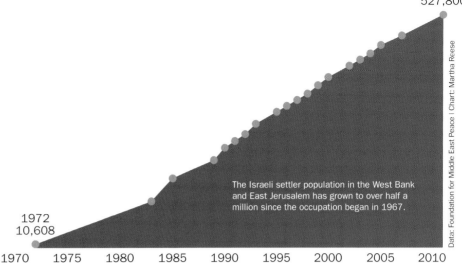

2011
527,800

1972
10,608

1970 1975 1980 1985 1990 1995 2000 2005 2010

The Israeli settler population in the West Bank and East Jerusalem has grown to over half a million since the occupation began in 1967.

Data: Foundation for Middle East Peace | Chart: Martha Reese

"When there is a fear or suspicion that a diplomatic process might actually take place, however unlikely that seems to outside observers, there is a tendency among settlement supporters within the government to try to speed things up."

Occasional attempts to uproot settlers are sensational media events, pitting fanatical religious-nationalist settlers against soldiers and police. These periodic demonstrations of government toughness have no effect in reducing the total settler population; removals of small encampments are portrayed as "painful concessions" that threaten the fabric of Israeli society—and the settlers often rebuild without interference outside the glare of media attention.

Riots ensued in December 2008 when settlers were forced to evacuate a building in Hebron they had occupied illegally. Prime Minister Ehud Olmert said, "Immediately after the evacuation, there were actions that cannot be described except as attempted pogroms by Jews from the Hebron area and other areas against Palestinian residents in Judea and Samaria. We are the children of a people whose historic ethos is built on the memory of pogroms....As a Jew, I am ashamed that Jews could do such a thing."

In a less-visible way, the Israeli land-grab of the Jordan Valley is already complete. Virtually all of the land in the Jordan Valley, other than actual built-up areas of the Palestinian population, is under the control of the settlements' regional councils (and off-limits to the Palestinians). Almost all of the Jordan Valley settlements, despite having tiny populations, nonetheless have huge footprints on the land, with extensive agricultural areas.

Sebastian Scheiner | AP

Left: Although all settlements in occupied territory are illegal under international law, Israel defines as illegal only "outposts" built without state planning permission. Israeli security forces demolish settlement outposts periodically, as happened in May 2009 at Maoz Esther, this hilltop site northeast of Ramallah. Such outposts are often rebuilt immediately without government interference and, over time, may be declared legitimate.

Below An armed fundamentalist West Bank settler threatens a Palestinian farmer harvesting her olives, April 2005. Palestinian victims of settler violence receive virtually no protection by Israeli police and army personnel. Israeli and international solidarity activists have documented criiminal settler activity, like this encounter witnessed by the International Women's Peace Service. Still, settlers are very rarely charged or punished for criminal violence against Palestinians and their property.

IWPS

Left: Sophisticated "terminals" like the Al Qader checkpoint give an appearance of normalcy to Israel's regime of movement restrictions. The ring road system of which this checkpoint is part isolates Jerusalem from its West Bank hinterland, fulfilling Israeli policies first formulated in the 1970s. As a result of decades of settlement construction, there are now more Israelis than Palestinians living in the Bethlehem Governate where the Gush Etzion settlement block is located; its two dozen Israeli settlements include Alon Shevut, Beitar Illit, Efrata, Neve Daniel, and Tekoa. This zone is also a major source of Palestinian water resources expropriated by Israel.

ISRAEL HAS SET up over 600 checkpoints, road-blocks, and segregated roads in the West Bank. The Israeli government claims checkpoints are necessary to prevent Palestinian attacks on Israelis, but checkpoints primarily restrict movement between Palestinian cities and villages, not between the Palestinian territories and Israel, at the same time preventing access to hospitals, schools, jobs, and farms.

Fixed checkpoints are permanent barriers manned by soldiers or police to restrict the free movement of pedestrians and vehicles, causing long delays. Abusive and humiliating confrontations often occur.

Random checkpoints (also known as "flying checkpoints") are temporary sites where the military and police stop pedestrians and vehicles to screen them for permits or to impede movement.

Roadblocks are concrete barriers, large stones, or high dirt piles that block the passage of vehicles on Palestinian roads. These barriers are usually unguarded and do not prevent people from crossing on foot, but they are a form of economic harassment because drivers are forced to transfer goods from a vehicle on one side of the roadblock to another on the other side. Instead of using their cars on the main road, Palestinians have to take indirect, unpaved roads or taxis that shuttle back and forth between road-

Above: Contrary to popular belief, the majority of checkpoints in the West Bank are not between the West Bank and Israel's internationally recognized borders, but rather within the Palestinian West Bank, most of them between Palestinian towns and villages.

Palestinian self-ruled areas (A and B), March 2000

Israeli cities and settlements, projected size, 2000

Existing or planned Israeli thoroughfares, 2000

A segregated network of roads built by Israel in the West Bank and linking it to Israel has consumed extensive tracts of Palestinian-owned land. These roads, while obscuring the border to Israelis, enable freedom of movement to settlers while inhibiting the movement of native Palestinians who are prohibited from using or crossing these roads.

Hessa lives in the village of Deir Ballut. At 2a.m. one morning when Hessa was seven months pregnant with twins, she started having contractions. She and her husband hastily made their way to the checkpoint outside their village to get a ride to the nearest hospital in Ramallah, 25 miles away. But the Israeli soldiers would not allow them to pass because the checkpoint is open only from 7a.m. to 7p.m. "Look, we didn't make the rules, and we don't even agree with them. We're just following orders," the soldiers explained. Hessa's husband pleaded with the soldiers for over two hours before they agreed to telephone their superiors for an exception to the rule. Before the ambulance could get to her, Hessa had given birth to premature twins. One died on the way to the hospital, the other at the hospital.

Restricted Movement

blocks, making even short distances difficult or impossible to cover quickly and efficiently.

Bypass roads (called "Lateral Roads" in the Oslo agreements) link settlements with one another and with Israel, circumventing Palestinian built-up areas. These roads include a 50- to 75-meter-wide buffer zone, in which no construction or planting is allowed. In effect, these roads—often constructed on expropriated Palestinian land—carve up the West Bank into isolated ghettos and often deprive Palestinians of vital agricultural land and the income from it.

As of August 2008, 493 miles of bypass roads were in use. These roads are restricted to Israelis with yellow license plates on their cars. Palestinian vehicles, identified by green license plates, are not allowed on these roads without a permit. Permits are difficult or impossible to obtain and expensive. Palestinian tranportation is relegated to inferior secondary roads that are, themselves, restricted by checkpoints and roadblocks.

The Israeli policy of dividing Palestine into fragmented, isolated cantons is based on the assumption that Israel's security needs justify not only control of its border with the territories, but the disruption of Palestinian life beyond the Green Line. In order that Israeli settlers may live in security and move freely, Palestinians live with little security and face sweeping restrictions on movement, a flagrant violation of international law.

Territorial expansion in the guise of security control drives the design of Israel's system of roads and barriers in the West Bank. The Israeli government's Settlement Master Plan for l983-86 states: "The road is the factor that motivates settlement…and [road] advancement will lead to development and demand." Clearly, easy vehicular access has been an attractive feature for settlers.

Instead of making Israel more secure, these policies undermine Israeli security by strengthening the Palestinian will to resist occupation and dispossession.

Above: An elderly Palestinian woman pleads with an Israeli soldier to let her cross the Ar-Ram checkpoint in January 2007. This incident, like hundreds of others, was photographically documented by the Israeli human rights organization Machsom Watch.

Below: A Machsom Watch member monitors the restriction on movement imposed by a cement-block barrier at the Kedar road in July 2005. For their work in documenting and sometimes intervening against abuses by the Israeli military at checkpoints, Machsom Watch's members—mostly Israeli women—have earned the respect of the Palestinians who seldom encounter sympathetic Israelis.

Left: Roadblocks like this one at Qarawat Bani Hassan in the Salfit region (see map on page 26) are set up and removed unpredictably, disrupting the transportation of Palestinian goods. The nearby village of Marda is served by three roads, but only one is open at any given time because of roadblocks. Palestinian goods are costly to transport since they must be carried by hand from truck to truck past roadblocks. As a result, Israeli products are often cheaper than their Palestinian counterparts, leaving captive-market Palestinian consumers a difficult choice between paying a premium for Palestinian products or subsidizing the occupier with their purchases.

The Wall

David Young

Mohammad Jalud lives in a village near Qalqilya on the east side of the wall. His fields are on the west side, just 10 minutes away, through a gate in the wall not open to Palestinians. After many applications he obtained a permit to enter a distant gate, but the trip to his fields then took one hour each way. Often he had to wait hours for the gate to be opened. Israeli officials refuse to allow him to take his tractor to his farm. He must carry all his farm implements and produce on his back, for even a donkey requires a permit. In 2005 he lost his entire crop because of these difficulties. If he takes a job and lets his land lie fallow, it will be confiscated under the Absentee Property Law.

In June 2002 the government of Israel began constructing a physical barrier to separate Israel and the West Bank. In most areas, the barrier is an electronic fence with Israel–only patrol zones, barbed-wire fences, and trenches on both sides, consuming a strip of land averaging 196 feet in width. In populated areas, a concrete wall 20 to 26 feet high has been erected.

The land on which the barrier is built is is not within Israel or on the border (the Green Line); it is on Palestinian land that Israel has occupied since the 1967 war.

The barrier has brought untold hardships for hundreds of thousands of Palestinians. The suffering has been particularly acute for those who depend on agriculture for their livelihoods. The land between the Green Line and the barrier is called the "seam zone" and is one of the most fertile areas of the West Bank. Along this seam zone thousands of Palestinians on both sides of the barrier are being driven into poverty by restrictions on residency, lack of access to farm lands, inability to market their crops, and confiscation of land. A small percentage of landowners living on the eastern side of the barrier are granted permits to farm land they own on the western side of the barrier.

When finished, the wall/barrier will usurp an additional 11.9% of Palestinian land in the West Bank. The agricultural Jordan Valley area— about 30% of the West Bank—is already off limits to Palestinians and has undergone a de-facto annexation to Israel.

Israel points to the dramatic decline in the number of suicide bombings since 2002 as justification for the barrier. Israel's right to defend its inhabitants from violence is undisputed; however, collective punishment of an entire population for the violent actions of a few is illegal. Furthermore, the route of the barrier does not separate Israel from the Palestinian territories but is situated to solidify the expropriation and annexation of Palestinian land for the construction and expansion of Jewish settlements which are, themselves, illegal.

The 1,800 residents of 'Azzun 'Atmeh are imprisoned in an enclave created by the Separation Barrier. In 2007 a resident who was injured in an accident died after soldiers at the barrier gate refused to allow his evacuation to a hospital in Qalqiliya.

Miki Kratsman | *Ha'aretz*

Above left: Uprooting olive trees in preparation for building another section of the separation barrier in the area of Bido Village, East Jerusalem.

Center: Since the barrier was constructed, Abd a-Latif 'Odeh has had to travel twenty-two kilometres from a-Dab'a village to reach his land, which is adjacent to his home, but on the other side of the fence.

Right: Expansion of the Modi'in Illit settlement block is enabled by expropriation of Palestinian land along the route of the separation barrier.

Kareem Jubran | B'Tselem (left and center)
Oren Ziv | Activestills (right)

Illegal

The International Court of Justice (ICJ) issued an advisory opinion in 2004 that Israel's building of a barrier in the occupied Palestinian territory is illegal and said construction must stop immediately and Israel should make reparations for any damage caused.

The judges found that the barrier's construction breaches international law, saying it violates principles outlined in the UN Charter and long-standing global conventions that prohibit the threat or use of force and the acquisition of territory by that means, as well as principles upholding the right of peoples to self-determination.

Observing that 80 per cent of Israeli settlers in the occupied Palestinian territory live between the barrier and the so-called Green Line marking the 1949 boundary of Israel, the Court said the structure's route could "prejudge the future frontier between Israel and Palestine."

The judges noted that, combined with the Israeli settlements, which have been deplored by the Security Council, the barrier's construction alters the demographic composition of the occupied Palestinian territory and impedes the Palestinians' right to self-determination.

Concluding that Israel could not rely on a right of self-defense or on a state of necessity to justify the barrier, the Court said it was not convinced the specific route chosen was necessary for security reasons.

Source: www.un.org/apps/news/story.asp?NewsID=11292&Cr=palestin&Cr1

The barrier cuts deep into the West Bank, stripping populated Palestinian areas of their surrounding agricultural land and freshwater aquifers, allocating both for Jewish settlements. Israel directly controls nearly half the territory of the West Bank and indirectly controls the rest. Palestinians are confined to the areas colored dark orange on the map at right.

Map legend:

- Barrier trajectory approved by Israel's Cabinet in April 2006
- Settlement areas east of the barrier
- Jordan Valley and Dead Sea slopes (Israeli controlled)
- ◣ Israeli settlements west of the barrier
- △ Settlements east of the barrier
- ---- Green Line, established 1949

Map: Foundation for Middle East Peace | www.fmep.org

West Bank (map labels): Rehan, Jenin, Khermesh, Mevo Dotan, Mehola, Tulkarm, Tubas, Maskiyot, Avne Hefez, Shave Shomron, Elon Moreh, Kedumim, Nablus, Hamra, Zufin, Brakha, Qalqilya, Yizhar, Itamar, A.Menashe, Oranit, Damiya Bridge (closed), Ariel, Massua, Salfit, Eli, Shilo, Ma'ale Efrayim, Bet Arieh, Halamish, Nili, Talmon, Bet El, Ofra, Modi'in Illit, Ramallah, G.Ze'ev, G.Binyamin, Jericho, Allenby Bridge, Ma'ale Adumim, Jerusalem, Betar Illit, Bethlehem, Tekoa, Efrat, K.Zur, Asfar, Adora, Hebron, Kiryat Arba, Otniel, Karmel, Eshkolot, Tene, Jordan River

Right: Israeli bulldozers arrived and began uprooting olive trees in the West Bank town of Kifil Haris (near Nablus) in December 2003. The army claimed to be expanding the settler road; other officials said they were excavating for a new water system; Haris's families feared the demolitions indicated that their village was on the planned route of the separation barrier. In the absence of official maps of the barrier's route, Palestinians find it difficult to mobilize resistance against demolitions.

Israeli outpost — Israeli settlement
Segregation Wall — Palestinian isolated land
Israeli bypass road
Palestinian built-up area — Kifil Haris village boundary
(#) Road number

Above: Within a few years of the bulldozers' destroying Kifil Haris' olive trees (top photo, this page), Israel's strategic objective had become apparent. Route 505, a new settler bypass road was constructed, splitting the village into two sections and isolating 1,100 acres of the village's lands. The separation barrier surrounding Ariel settlement bloc consolidates this expropriation. Already 133 acres of the village's lands have been confiscated and allocated to Ariel. See map at www.poica.org/editor/case_studies/KH_08.jpg.

Right: On October 11, 2008, the residents of Burin and nearby villages went to harvest olives in their fields, next to which the settlement of Yitzhar was established in 1984. While harvesting they were attacked by settlers who threw stones at the Palestinians and damaged their olive trees. There is a history of violence between villagers and the settlement's Orthodox Jewish residents, who currently number about 500. The settlement is located deep inside the occupied Palestinian territories near Nablus.

Environmental Occupation

As olive trees are uprooted, so are Palestinians' lives

A MILLION AND A quarter trees and thousands of acres of farmland have been destroyed in Palestinian territories by Israelis since 1967. Nearly 465,000 olive trees were uprooted between 2000 and 2005, and the destructive practices continue to the present time.

Destruction of agricultural tracts is perpetrated in two forms: Israeli military actions in support of state land expropriation and destructive vandalism by Jewish settlers.

Palestinians face draconian restrictions on the movement of people and goods in the territories. Many Palestinian farmers cannot reach their agricultural lands to tend and harvest their crops because of road closures. The separation barrier has deepened the agricultural crisis, permanently separating Palestinian families from their farmlands, except for locked, unmanned gates that allow unpredictable access.

Under a law from the Ottoman era, Israel claims as state property land that has been "abandoned" and left uncultivated for four years. This land is then usually declared Israeli state land and often later allocated to Israeli settlements for expansion. By making it almost impossible for some farmers to get to their land, Israel can claim that Palestinian land has been "abandoned." Often, land expropriation is effected without resort to even such bureaucratic chicanery as this.

Olive trees are a major source of livelihood for many Palestinian

The occupation's manifest harm to the environment is pervasive and profound. Its effects encompass a broad spectrum of hazards from overextraction of groundwater, to the effect of the Wall on rainwater runoff and animal migration, to infrastructural restrictions on the Palestinians' own capacity for rubbish disposal, to the dumping of settlement rubbish and sewage on Palestinian agricultural land, as shown in this 2005 photo taken at Deir Sharaf.

families. By targeting olive trees, the Israeli government is sabotaging the Palestinian economy.

World Bank reports have condemned the uprooting of olive trees as violating the trade policies of the Paris protocols of 1954 which calls for "free access for Palestinian goods to the Israeli market and vice versa." Property destruction also violates Article 33 of the Fourth Geneva Convention, which prohibits collective punishment.

Israel's control of water supply leaves Palestinians thirsty

SINCE THE BEGINNING of the occupation in 1967, Israel's strict control of the water sector in the occupied territories has prevented development to meet Palestinian water needs, and caused shortages and a water-quality crisis.

Water in the occupied Palestinian territories has been fully incorporated into the Israeli water-management system to the general benefit of Israel and detriment of Palestinians. About 70% of groundwater on which Israel is dependent and 40% of its annual fresh water supply originate in the occupied territories. Of the water available from West Bank aquifers, Israel uses 73%, West Bank Palestinians use 17%, and illegal Jewish settlements use 10%. As a result, West Bank Palestinian water consumption is 40 liters per day less than the minimum global standards set by the World Health Organization (WHO).

Israel is in control of all water development in the West Bank. Israel can veto any Palestinian requests to drill wells or collect surface water. It is difficult if not impossible for Palestinians in occupied territories to get permission to drill a new water well or even repair one. Because of the water shortage, many Palestinians have to buy water from tankers; poor families spend up to one-fifth of their income on water.

Gaza's water crisis is even more profound than that in the West Bank. The aquifer that provides 96% of water consumed in the Gaza Strip has become polluted and salinated by over-extraction and penetration of untreated sewage and agricultural runoff. Only 7% of the water in the Gaza Strip meets WHO standards. The siege and blockade imposed by Israel since 2006 has made maintenance of infrastructure nearly impossible; the winter war of 2008-2009 shattered Gaza's already-failing water treatment and delivery capacity.

Israel has neglected construction of infrastructure to connect the Palestinian rural population to a running-water network as well as proper maintenance of existing networks. In 2008, 227,500 Palestinians in 220 towns and villages were not connected to a water network. Another 190,000 Palestinians are only partially served.

In the West Bank, about 50 groundwater wells and more than 200 cisterns have been destroyed or isolated from their owners by construction of the separation barrier, affecting the domestic and agricultural needs of more than 122,000 people.

> "Although [Israelis and Palestinians] share the mountain aquifer that runs the length of the occupied West Bank, Palestinians have access to only a fifth of the water supply, while Israel, which controls the area, takes the rest.
>
> —Rory McCarthy, *The Guardian*, May 27, 2009

Shareef Sarhan

During the offensive that flattened homes, government buildings, schools, clinics, and refugee camps, the Israeli Defense Ministry closed Israel's border crossings with Gaza and prevented the delivery of United Nations aid shipments. The UN condemned the closure and warned Israel against imposing illegal "collective punishment" against Gaza's 1.5 million residents, most of whom depend on foreign aid. "The Israeli reaction is not justified by those rocket attacks, even though it's caused by those rocket attacks," said John Holmes, undersecretary-general for Humanitarian Affairs.

Today's horrific attacks mark only a change in Israel's method of killing Palestinians....In recent months they died mostly silent deaths, the elderly and sick especially, deprived of food and necessary medicine by the two-year-old Israeli blockade calculated and intended to cause suffering and deprivation to 1.5 million Palestinians, the vast majority refugees and children....In Gaza, Palestinians died silently, for want of basic medications... prohibited from reaching them by Israel.

—Ali Abunimah, Electronic Intifada, December 27, 2008

THE FIRST STRIKE in Israel's Operation "Cast Lead" occurred on December 27, 2008, when 60 Israeli F-16 fighter jets bombed 50 sites in Gaza, killing over 200 Palestinians and wounding close to 1,000 more. During the next 22 days Israel unleashed its full arsenal including phosphorous bombs and cluster bombs on a trapped and largely defenseless civilian population. The ferocity of the attack on civilians and militants alike and the magnitude of the devastation shocked the world.

Shareef Sa

Markets were bombed, farms destroyed. Medical personnel including ambulance drivers were targeted and prevented from evacuating the wounded. Civilian and military areas were targeted, seemingly indiscriminately. As the Israeli assault drew to a close on January 17, demolition squads destroyed all the factories in the northern part of Gaza City.

Israeli officials announced two objectives of the war: to stop Hamas from firing Qassam rockets into Israel, and to eradicate Hamas altogether by killing its militia. Some analysts doubted these stated objectives; a truce between Israel and Hamas had already put an end to Hamas rocket fire. It was recorded that Israel broke the truce on November 4, 2008, by killing six Hamas militia, thus inciting Hamas to resume its rocket fire.

The Gaza war in statistics

- 1,400 Palestinians killed, including at least 850 civilians, 350 children, and 110 women; over 5,000 wounded

- 14 Israelis killed, including 4 civilians, 330 wounded

- Over 4,000 homes destroyed, over 40,000 damaged

- 215 factories and 700 private businesses seriously damaged or destroyed

- 15 hospitals and 43 primary health care centers destroyed or damaged

- 28 government buildings and 60 police stations destroyed or damaged

- 30 mosques destroyed, 28 damaged

- 10 schools destroyed and 168 damaged; three universities/colleges destroyed and 14 damaged

- 53 United Nations properties damaged

Approximately 80% of Gaza's Palestinians are the descendants of the 1948 Nakba from what is now southern Israel—the area of Israel that has come under fire from Gaza militants' home-made Qassam rockets. In the decades since the wars that caused their initial exodus from Israel, many Palestinians have become homeless again during Israeli incursions and home demolitions in Gaza.

War on Gaza

Hamas' Qassam rockets are inaccurate and contain explosive charges that are small compared to what is contained in a single Israeli shell. From 2004 until the beginning of Operation Cast Lead in December 2008, Hamas launched over 8,000 rockets and mortars killing 20 Israelis. By contrast, between 2000 and December 26, 2008 (prior to the 2008-2009 war on Gaza), 3,000 Palestinians in Gaza were killed by Israel forces. [Source: B'Tselem]

For six months during its truce with Hamas, Israel was planning a war on two fronts—the battlefield and the world press. An opportune moment to launch came during the 2008–2009 Christmas/New Year holiday, which coincided with the Bush–Obama presidential transition.

Commentators around the world asked what military advantage was served by killing and maiming civilians and extensive property destruction. Why would the fourth most powerful military in the world seek to destroy the institutions of an imprisoned group of refugees? Perhaps the best clue to Israel's gradual strangulation of the Palestinian people over the past 42 years comes from a remark attributed to Moshe Yaalon, Israeli Defense Forces Chief of Staff in 2002. "The Palestinians must be made to understand in the deepest recesses of their consciousness that they are a defeated people."

On January 22, 2009, Richard Falk, the UN Special Rapporteur—and himself a Jew—declared that Israel's actions against the besieged Gazans were reminiscent of "the worst kind of international memories of the Warsaw Ghetto," a reference to the starvation and murder of Polish Jews by the Nazis. The world is reminded of Israeli historian Ilan Pappe's description of Israeli actions as "a creeping transfer in the West Bank, and a measured genocidal policy in the Gaza strip...."

> How ironic that the [Gaza refugee] camps, a product of Israel's racist, ethnic cleansing policies, are now the principal breeding ground of the extremist groups against which Israel "has a right to defend itself."
>
> —Donald K. McInnes, Unitarian Universalists for Justice in the Middle East

The Fatah–Hamas power struggle and the Gaza blockade

Beginning in the late 1980s, Israel and the US worked covertly to establish and support Hamas in order to weaken Yasser Arafat. When Hamas candidates won a majority of the seats in the Palestinian parliament in the January 2006 elections, Israel quickly arrested 42 of them—and still holds them in prison. Israel also sealed Gaza in a maneuver to isolate and topple Hamas. Dov Weisglas, advisor to the Israeli Prime Minister, explained that "the idea is to put the Palestinians on a diet, but not make them die of hunger."

In spite of Hamas' election victory in a free and fair election, the US and the EU joined in the boycott of Hamas, demanding that Hamas renounce all violence and recognize Israel's right to exist, but making no reciprocal demands on Israel.

In June 2007, after it became clear that Israel and the US were arming and training elements in Fatah for a military putsch against the elected government, Hamas staged a pre-emptive coup and ousted Fatah militants from Gaza—more than 350 militants died in the skirmishes. Since then several attempts at political unity between the parties have failed. In the meantime, Israel has tightened its blockade of Gaza, depriving the Strip of food, medicines, electricity, fuel, building supplies, and most other necessities.

Palestinians pray on their land prior to the weekly demonstration against the apartheid wall in the West Bank village of Ni'lin, April 10, 2009. Residents of Ni'lin have already lost hundreds of acres to Israeli settlements. The wall would confiscate another 25% of their land.

Oren Ziv | Activestills

ALMOST TWO-THIRDS of the estimated nine million Palestinians in the world are refugees or displaced people, the result of massive violence against the Palestinian people. The ethnic cleansing of Palestinian villages and towns at Israel's founding, the demolition of thousands of homes in the decades since, and the tragic statistics on civilian deaths and injuries over years of occupation are ample evidence of the brutality of Israeli policies.

Resistance to oppression is often viewed in the absence of its context, then portrayed as inexplicable barbarity. Some forms of resistance to oppression and colonization are approved in the United Nations charter and in international law and must be distinguished from real terrorism. In the context of the Palestinian struggle for self-determination, this distinction between legitimate resistance and terrorism has been intentionally obfuscated for political ends. In most cases, the media call Palestinian armed resistance "terrorism" while all attacks on Palestinians by the Israeli army are named "self-defense." Little notice is taken of the fact that terror can be "from above" (by the state) and "from below" (by those who resist the violence of the state).

The right of armed resistance to tyranny is a part of the Reformed Tradition and is enshrined in the US Declaration of Independence, as well as various UN resolutions and customary international laws which affirm the legitimacy of armed resistance. UNGA A/RES/33/24 of November 29, 1978, "Reaffirms the legitimacy of the struggle of peoples for independence, territorial integrity, national unity, and liberation from colonial and foreign domination and foreign occupation by all available means, particularly armed struggle." The principle of self-determination itself provides that, in certain circumstances, force may be used in response to force in the pursuit of self-determination.

Some Palestinian resistance has, indeed, taken forms defined as illegal and illegitimate under international law. In the context of 61 years of ethnic cleansing and violence targeting the Palestinian people collectively, the number of Palestinians engaging in violent resistance is smaller than might be expected. It must be said, however,

Resistance to Occupation

Yotam Ronen | Activestills

Yotam Ronen | Activestills

The agricultural village of Bil'in lies 16 km west of Ramallah. Land belonging to the village has been confiscated in successive stages starting in the 1980s as Jewish settlements were established in the vicinity: Matityahu, Kiryat Sefer, Modi'in Illit, and Matityahu East. In April 2004 Israel began construction of the annexation barrier on the western side of the village, expropriating for its route about 2,300 hectares (575 acres) of Bil'in land.

In response, the people of Bil'in, under the leadership of resident Iyad Burnat, mobilized a campaign of nonviolent resistance involving weekly Friday demonstrations. International and Israeli activists have since joined the campaign in significant numbers. The resistance at Bi'lin is now in its seventh year; similar initiatives are taking place in Ni'lin, Jayyous, and other villages threatened by land expropriation.

The people of Bil'in have pursued legal options as well. Represented by Michael Sfard, an Israeli human rights lawyer, the village entered a petition to the Israel high court in 2005. The court ruling required the Israeli government to reroute the barrier to expropriate less of the village's land. Such qualified legal "victories" are the exception to the rule and, at that, have minimal impact on the ongoing Israeli land-grab.

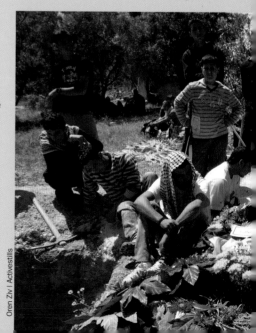

Left top: Palestinian demonstrators and their Israeli and international allies face Israeli soldiers at a weekly demonstration in Bil'in in August 2005. More than six years later, the demonstrations continue.

Left bottom: Demonstrators run from a teargas cloud shot by the Israeli army during a protest against the apartheid wall in Bil'in on February 20, 2009—the fourth anniversary of the start of protests.

Oren Ziv | Activestills

Some 100 Palestinian demonstrators in Jayyous, joined by Israeli and international activists, march towards the apartheid wall that separates the village from most of its land, November 16, 2008. Farmers are allowed to reach their land only after getting permission from the Israeli army.

Yotam Ronen | Activestills

that such actions have caused grievous harm to individual Israelis and rightly drawn near-universal condemnation, including condemnation by Palestinian Christian theologians. (E.g., see Naim Ateek, *Suicide Bombers: What is theologically and morally wrong with suicide bombing?*" Sabeel, 2003.)

Palestinian attempts to gain redress through access to the international bodies that exist for the nonviolent resolution of disputes, including the International Court of Justice and the United Nations, have been stymied, often by US and Israeli combined intransigence. Palestinians have been deprived of legal remedy despite the weight of evidence compiled by international human rights monitoring organizations.

The prepondenance of resistance against Israel's domination has been and is being undertaken by nonviolent means. And yet, the legacy of Palestinian nonviolent resistance is little known—while sensational acts of

terrorism have received relentless attention and define the struggle in the minds of many people unfamiliar with the actuality. Civilian resistance including petitions, strikes, civil disobedience, noncooperation, and boycotts first emerged in the 1920s against the British occupation of Mandate Palestine and its encouragement of Zionist colonial settlement. As early as 1936, Palestinian Christian and Muslim religious leaders were imprisoned for dissenting from Palestine's transformation into a Jewish state. Land Day, begun in 1976 in response to confiscation by the Israeli government of Palestinian land in Galilee, is now observed annually by Palestinian exiles

around the world. The tax revolt of the first intifada began in 1989 in Beit Sahour. The Israeli government has taken many actions to undercut such programs of non-violence, jailing their leaders and forcing others to leave. While many have decried the absence of a "Palestinian Gandhi," the fact is that many are struggling valiantly against heavy odds to be precisely that.

Today, Palestinians whose West Bank villages lie along the path of the separation barrier are engaged in innovative forms of nonviolent resistance in villages, often with the support of Israeli and international allies. Resistance includes "sumud," an Arabic word meaning "steadfastness." Although Israel has intentionally made it difficult to remain on their ancestral lands, Palestinians resist flight and despair by merely surviving day by day with dignity and maintaining a strong social fabric under conditions of profound, chronic stress.

People around the world are acting in support of Palestinian nonviolent resistance to occupation. Since the governments of many western nations support Israeli oppression with financial assistance and diplomatic influence, a global movement for boycotts, divestment, and sanctions has been initiated.

In July 2008 Bil'in commenced legal proceedings in Canadian courts against Green Park International Inc. and Green Mount International Inc., two Canadian corporations involved in the construction, marketing, and sale of settlement housing units in Modi'in Illit.

Oren Ziv | Activestills

Above: Israeli soldiers arrest a Palestinian man who tried to block them from shooting tear gas canisters toward the crowd of demonstrators during a protest against the apartheid wall in Bil'in on April 24, 2009. Hundreds of Palestinians, Israelis, and internationals protested the murder of Bassam Ibrahim Abu Rahma, who was killed by an Israeli solider during the Friday demonstration a week earlier.

Left: Friends of Bassam Ibrahim Abu Rahma gather at his grave after his funeral in Bil'in on April 18, 2009. Abu Rahma, 30, was killed in a confrontation with Israeli border policemen during a protest on April 17 after being shot with an extended-range teargas projectile aimed directly at his chest at close range. He was critically injured and died shortly after arriving at a hospital in Ramallah.

> The context that is often missing from the current reporting is that the Palestinian uprising is a revolt against a 34-year-long occupation. If there is no occupation in the story, then the story doesn't really make sense.
>
> —Alisa Solomon, *Peace, Propaganda and the Promised Land*, 2001

Part Three: Responses

Over the past three or four decades, in spite of Israel's illegal occupation and confiscation of Palestinian land, the United States has provided unwavering diplomatic and financial support for Israel. At first the Obama administration signaled an intention to change course, but the repeated humiliations it has suffered at the hands of the Netanyahu government and the Israel Lobby demonstrate that any meaningful alteration of the facts on the ground is not likely to happen without grassroots engagement by Americans whose taxes support the Israeli occupation and whose votes elect the politicians who determine our foreign policy.

The Presbyterian Church (U.S.A.) has a longstanding commitment to peacemaking activities in Palestine/Israel on multiple fronts, including ameliorating the conditions of Palestinians' lives and advocating for a just peace. These activities and relationships have been sustained by General Assembly resolutions dating from 1948 forward, by program funds to support personnel and programs in the Holy Land, and by participation in the ecumenical bodies of the Middle East.

" Since 1948, the Presbyterian Church General Assembly has called repeatedly for a just peace that respects the rights and needs of both Israelis and Palestinians. The Amman Call of 2007 demands of us a fresh commitment. Palestinian Christians—from Gaza to Jerusalem to Nazareth—are urging us as their brothers and sisters in Christ to act with speed and determination. "Enough is enough," they say. "No more words without deeds. It is time for action."

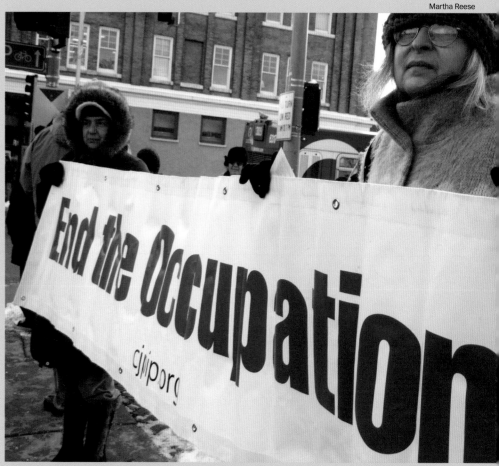

Martha Reese

As awareness grows, more individuals and organizations committed to the pursuit of just peace for Palestinians and Israelis find constructive ways of engagement. In the United States, Presbyterians are working within the church and building bridges with others in actions like this vigil in protest of Israel's siege and assault of Gaza. The vigil, which took place on January 19, 2009, in Oak Park, Illinois, brought together Christians, Jews, Muslims, and others and drew some 75 participants.

The economics of the occupation

The US role in sustaining the Israeli occupation

O N MAY 18, 2009, President Obama and Israeli Prime Minister Binyamin Netanyahu met at the White House to discuss the conditions necessary for peace in the Middle East. The result was a clash of world views between the two governments—the first major clash in many years.

The US relationship with Israel has been one in which the US has turned a blind eye to Israel's breach of international law and negotiated agreements with the Palestinians.

Political pressure from military contractors, oil companies, construction and high-tech companies, neo-conservative ideologues, Christian Zionists, and the "Israel Lobby" have

President George W. Bush (shown here with Knesset speaker Dalia Itzik) traveled in May 2008 to Israel to mark its 60th anniversary. Bush addressed a special session of the Israeli parliament, affirming that the United States was "proud to be Israel's closest ally and best friend." Historically, the US-Israel "special relationship" has taken the form of uncritical diplomatic support and unrestricted funding.

Safad | EPA

combined to provide almost unconditional support in Congress for whatever the Israeli government says and does. No US president to date has been able to to consistently or effectively resist that pressure for long.

The US diplomatic monopoly of the conflict serves to advance Israel's goals. Diplomatic protection buffers Israel from international scrutiny and

perpetuates the "peace process gridlock" that allows the Israeli government to negotiate indefinitely while intensifying the occupation.

Military aid to Israel

In the mid-1960s, US aid to Israel averaged $63 million per year; by 1971 the annual allocation was increased ten-fold to $634.5 million; after the Yom Kippur War in 1973, Congress bumped up US aid to over $3 billion per year. In recent years the level has remained at $3 billion in direct assistance. This amounts to one-sixth of all US foreign aid and 2% of the Israeli budget. On average, the US gave more than $6.8 million to Israel *each day* during 2007.

At present, aid takes the form of military aid. At the end of the fiscal year, the US Congress often converts that year's loans to Israel into grants. Every other country is required to account for how US aid is spent—not Israel.

US aid has been used to support Israel's military occupation of Palestine, to build illegal colonies and segregated highways on Palestinian lands, to construct what Palestinians call the apartheid wall, to pulverize Lebanon in 1982 and again in 2006, and devastate West Bank cities in 2002. The primary weapons used in the Israeli assault on Gaza in December-January 2008-2009 were American-made: F-16s, Blackhawk and Apache helicopters, and Caterpillar D-9 bulldozers.

In August 2007 the Bush Administration announced a new ten-year agreement that it would increase US military assistance to Israel by $6 billion over the next decade.

Palestinians see a blatant double standard in US diplomatic and financial support for Israel's occupation. The security pretext for Israel's annexation/apartheid barrier obscures the daily fact of the occupation. In depriving its victims of their human rights, freedom, and dignity, the occupation is itself an extreme form of violence and oppression, to which Palestinian violence is an understandable response.

> During negotiations, [the United States] rarely if ever adopt[s] objectively neutral or equidistant positions between Israel and the Arabs. Indeed, we often operate on peace process software that automatically adjusts our position in light of Israel's needs and concerns....This pro-Israel posture makes us a partial mediator.

—Aaron David Miller, Middle East analyst, author, and negotiator, *The Long Dance: Searching for Arab-Israeli Peace*, Woodrow Wilson International Center for Scholars

Diplomatic support for the occupation

Since 1972 the US has vetoed over 43 UN Security Council resolutions criticizing Israel for breaches of international law. The US Congress frequently passes resolutions in support of Israeli military actions like attacks in Lebanon in 2002 and 2006 and the attack on Gaza in 2008—offensives that mock the moral principle of proportionality and outrage much of the rest of the world.

Furthermore, the US has turned a blind eye to Israel's 200 or so nuclear weapons and put no pressure on Israel to permit site inspections of its nuclear facilities. Nor has the US condemned Israel's active chemical and biological weapons program. It is as though different rules apply to Israel alone.

In light of what has transpired over

> Without concrete consequences for Tel Aviv's noncompliance—such as withholding all or part of the $3 billion annual US military aid to Israel, or withdrawing the US diplomatic protection that keeps Israel from being held accountable in the UN Security Council—Obama's demands for a settlement freeze or anything else will have little impact.

—Phyllis Bennis, Z Space, June 17, 2009

Israeli Prime Minister Binyamin Netanyahu poses for an official photograph with US Secretary of State Hillary Clinton following a press conference at the Prime Minister's office in Jerusalem on October 31, 2009.

Palestinian policymakers—along with many other observers—fault the Obama administration for its unwillingness to demand Israel's compliance with US policy directives. Nowhere is the discrepancy between established US policy and Israeli actions more obvious than in Israel's ongoing creation and expansion of settlements built on occupied land.

In an ABC News interview taped on February 18, 2011, US Secretary of State Hillary Clinton reiterated that "...it's been American policy for many years that [Israeli] settlements were illegitimate...."

Nevertheless, later the same day, US Ambassador Susan Rice vetoed a United Nations Security Council resolution condemning continued Israeli settlement expansion as illegal. The United States was the sole opponent to the resolution based on US policy positions; the 14 other Security Council members voted in favor. The US veto flies in the face of the body of international law that unambiguously defines settlement construction as illegal.

Statements by Secretary Clinton and others in the Obama administration criticizing Israeli settlement-building activity have gone unheeded by the Netanyahu government. Aid to Israel is not conditional on compliance. Millions of dollars in US military aid flow unimpeded while the US wields its veto in the United Nations to shield Israel from international condemnation.

Such actions foster justifiable cynicism throughout the world about the ability of the US to function as an unbiased intermediary in peace talks between Palestinians and Israelis.

the past 44 years, it is hard to dispute the charge that the US has not been an honest broker between Israelis and Palestinians. Many have concluded that change in the "facts on the ground" in Israel/Palestine will occur only when the "facts on the ground" in the US are changed.

Socially responsible economic engagement

THE PRESBYTERIAN CHURCH (U.S.A.) has been a leader in the field of socially responsible investment since the early 1970s with the creation of a special committee on Mission Responsibility through Investment (MRTI). The church studies where and how its money is used and takes action to promote better corporate practices through corporate engagement.

Since 1967, many Israeli and international corporations have made huge profits from the military occupation of Palestinian land. Corporations profit from the occupation whenever they do business in illegal settlements. Many Americans are not aware that companies as well known as Blockbuster and Ace Hardware do business in such large, suburban-style cities as Ma'ale Adumim, an illegal settlement built on Palestinian land deep inside the West Bank. Nor are they aware that the incentives that bring these businesses into the heart of illegal occupation are often underwritten by American tax dollars.

Corporations also profit from the construction of illegal settlements, the infrastructure that supports them, and the barriers that claim Palestinian land for Israel. For example, Hewlett Packard owns a company that provides monitoring at checkpoints inside the West Bank. Ingersoll Rand provides hand scanners used in these checkpoints. Terex provides lighting and construction equipment for building the wall and settlements.

Two American companies that the PC(USA) MRTI Committee is engaging to end their role in the occupation are Caterpillar and Motorola.

CAT equipment has demolished thousands of homes, uprooted countless olive trees, and carved gaping holes in Palestinian roads to make them impassable. In addition, CAT equipment is used in the construction of settlement housing, segregated roads on expropriated land, and the annexation/apartheid barrier—all violations of international law.

StolenBeauty.org promotes a boycott of Ahava beauty products because the Dead Sea minerals used in the firm's formulas are produced in the illegal West Bank settlement of Mitzpe Shalem using natural ingredients taken from Palestinian sources.

While Israel defends its right to "natural growth" in expanding settlements built on occupied territory, tens of thousands of Palestinian houses in East Jerusalem and the West Bank face demolition because they were built without a permit. Building permits are nearly impossible for Palestinians to obtain. This bureaucratic formula for circumscribing "natural growth" in Palestinian communities gives Israel's practice of bulldozing Palestinian homes a veneer of legitimacy because only "illegal" houses are demolished. The armored D-9 Caterpillar seen here is used in military actions and provided to Israel as a part of the US Pentagon's Foreign Military Financing program.

The challenge to corporations: "Stop profiting from occupation!"

Corporations that profit from Israel's occupation are under pressure to change. Dozens of major companies have faced protests, lost contracts, and seen their products removed from store shelves and university campuses as their role in perpetuating the conflict is exposed. This pressure is coming from many religious organizations, coalitions, human rights groups, institutions, and businesses. Below is a sampling of organizations that have called for corporate engagement **CE**, divestment **D**, boycott **B**, or government sanctions **S** to end Israel's occupation. It shows how this movement is growing throughout the US and the global community.

2004
- The 216th General Assembly of the Presbyterian Church (U.S.A.) **CE/D**

2005
- 170 Palestinian coalitions and human rights groups **BDS**
- Church of Ireland **D**
- S. African Council of Churches **B**
- World Council of Churches **D**
- United Methodist Virginia and New England Conferences **D**

2006
- Church of England Synod **D**
- Canadian Union of Public Employees, Ontario (200,000 members) **D**
- Congress of South African Trade Unions (1.2 million members) **BDS**
- ASN Bank (Dutch) **B**

2007
- Irish Congress of Trade Unions (832,000 members) **D**
- British Union of Journalists **B**

2008
- London School of Economics Students' Union **D**
- Canadian Union of Postal Workers (50,000 members) **BDS**
- United Church of Canada Toronto Assembly **B**
- 218th General Assembly, PC(USA) **CE/D**

2009
- Hampshire College **D**
- Pashima (British textiles) **B**
- BlackRock (investments) **D**
- PFZW (Dutch pension fund) **D**
- Palestinian Christian Kairos Document (endorsed by Bishops and Patriarchs) **BDS**
- British Trade Union Congress (6.5 million members!!) **BDS**

2010
- 219th General Assembly, PC(USA): Denouncement of Caterpillar, Inc.
- Israel Palestine Mission Network, PC(USA) **BDS**
- Danske Bank **D**
- United Methodist Church, Detroit Conference and Northern Illinois Conference **D**
- Methodist Church of Britain **B**
- Australian National Council of Churches **B**
- South Africa Council of Churches **BDS**
- COOP Italian supermarkets **B**
- Nordiconad Italian supermarkets **B**
- Norwegian Government Pension Fund **D**
- Scottish Trade Union Congress (640,000 members) **BDS**
- Evergreen State College Student Body **D**

2011
- United Methodist General Board of Church & Society **D**
- Edinborough University student body **BDS**

Jewish and Israeli Groups
- A Different Jewish Voice (Netherlands)
- Jewish Voice for Peace (US)
- Jewish Voice for a Just Peace in Middle East (Germany)
- Critical Jewish Voice (Austria)
- Women's International League for Peace & Freedom (Israel)
- Int'l. Jewish Anti-Zionist Network
- American Jews for a Just Peace
- Israeli Committee Against House Demolitions (Israel)
- European Jews for a Just Peace
- Independent Jewish Voices (Canada)
- Australian Jewish Democratic Society
- New Profile (Israel)
- Rete-ECO (Italy)
- Union Juive Française Pour la Paix (France)
- Coalition of Women for Peace (Israel)
- Jews for Justice for Palestinians (UK)
- Boycott from Within (Israel)
- Not in Our Name (Argentina)
- Meretz USA (selective boycott)

This Soda Club factory is located within the West Bank settlement industrial zone of Mishor Adumim. Soda Club (also known as SodaStream) is a publicly traded company: NASDAQ:SODA. A full analysis is available at www.whoprofits.org/articlefiles/WhoProfits-ProductioninSettlements-SodaStream.pdf

SodaStream home beverage carbonating devices are widely available in the US at Bed Bath & Beyond, Bloomingdales, Macy's, Sears, Kmart, and elsewhere.

Anti-occupation demonstrators gather outside Motorola offices in New York City on March 30, 2009, calling for a boycott of Motorola products.

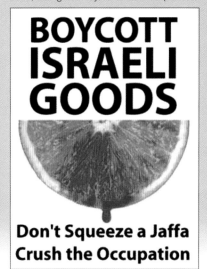

BOYCOTT ISRAELI GOODS

Don't Squeeze a Jaffa Crush the Occupation

Caterpillar's weaponized bulldozers were used to clear the way for ground troops in Israel's 2008-09 assault on the Gaza Strip. The IDF considers these bulldozers such an important part of its weaponry that it has announced plans to draft civilians to maintain them on the battlefield. The Goldstone Report on human rights violations cited the testimony of Israeli soldiers who witnessed the mass demolition of Palestinian homes "all the way to the sea" by CAT bulldozers during Operation Cast Lead.

Calls for boycott, divestment, and sanctions (BDS) are a direct result of Israel's actions against Palestinians.

BDS is supported by growing numbers of people of every faith around the world who seek a just and lasting peace, including Palestinians and many Israelis.

Many have concluded that non-violent economic pressure is the only effective way to change corporate behavior and government policies. Certainly this was the case in South Africa, where global efforts to end apartheid continued for years before divestment from companies cooperating with that government finally ended the oppression.

Even those who believe divestment and boycotts are ineffective must

As an aid to consumers wishing to boycott Israeli exports produced in settlements in the occupied territories, the Israeli organization Gush Shalom maintains a list on its website. Vegetables, fruit, and flowers constitute a major part of settlement exports, but, Gush Shalom notes, "they are usually mixed with products made in Israel, so...locating the exact origin of such products is nearly impossible." Some activists, including www.bigcampaign.org, advocate a South Africa-style boycott of all Israeli goods, not just those traceable to settlements.

acknowledge a moral choice: They can continue to profit from Israel's occupation through companies that sustain it, or redirect their funds to other companies. The churches led in the struggle against apartheid; now the world watches to see whether churches put actions behind their words on behalf of justice in Palestine.

Post-Gaza: a new chapter in the quest for just peace

Since the Gaza war ended, numerous projects—organized collaboratively by international activists, Palestinians, and Israelis—have drawn international attention to the disastrous consequences of military occupation on the lives of Palestinians in Gaza, the West Bank, and East Jerusalem. In this photo, thousands of participants in the Gaza Freedom March massed in Cairo with water purification, school, and medical supplies. The March, held on the first anniversary of the Israeli military assault on Gaza that occurred during winter 2008-09, sought to relieve dire shortages faced by Gaza's 1.5 million residents brought on by the blockade of the territory enforced by Israel and Egypt.

I N THE TURBULENT MONTHS since the cessation of outright warfare in Gaza, some analysts have lamented that a mutually agreeable negotiated settlement to the Israeli-Palestinian conflict seems more remote than ever before. At the same time, Palestinian, Israeli, and international activists are undertaking dramatic, inspiring actions with an unprecedented degree of international coordination, while some leaders and human rights monitoring organizations have vigorously condemned Israeli abuses and intransigence.

Israel moves farther to the right

The world outcry against the War on Gaza shocked many Israelis and catapulted hardliner Binyamin Netanyahu into leadership during the February 2009 elections. In order to form a coalition government, Netanyahu picked cabinet members who were even farther to the right of his own right-wing Likud Party, including Foreign Minister Avigdor Lieberman.

During 2009 and 2010 the Knesset and the Netanyahu government introduced over 20 new laws and bills discriminating against Palestinian citizens of Israel and Israeli human rights organizations.[1]

One of the most notorious is the October 2010 Loyalty Oath approved by the Netanyahu cabinet in a vote of 22 to 8. It is discriminatory by design, requiring those seeking Israeli citizenship to pledge allegiance to "the state of Israel as a Jewish and democratic state," a Zionist state ideology that would exclude Palestinians and make their opposition to Israel's

system of discriminatory laws an act of treason. Also ominous is the approval by the Constitution, Law, and Justice Committee of the Knesset of a bill on February 14, 2011, making it illegal to initiate or incite boycotts against Israeli individuals, companies, factories, and organizations.[2] B'Tselem calls attacks like these a "witch hunt," "reminiscent of America's McCarthyite past" which undermines "the essential role of criticism within a healthy democracy."[3] As if to prove B'Tselem's point, the Knesset passed the Elkin Law on February 21, 2011. Its goal is to delegitimize Israeli human rights organizations that seek to influence public policy, while giving a free pass to hard-line foreign private donors who seek to shape Israel policy.[4]

Frank, public expressions of anti-Arab racism appear to be on the rise among Israeli Jewish religious leaders. A letter signed in December 2010 by dozens of municipal chief rabbis (whose salaries are paid from public funds) instructed their followers not to rent or sell property to non-Jews. A short time later, 30 wives of prominent rabbis issued a letter urging young women, "do not go out with non-Jews, don't work in places with non-Jews, and don't do national service together with non-Jews."[5]

In the West Bank and East Jerusalem violence against Palestinians by settlers is sometimes justified in religious terms. Rabbi Yitzhak Shapira, one of the leading ideologues of the extreme wing of the religious settler movement and resident of the extremist West Bank settlement Yitzhar, champions the "price tag" policy, which inflicts attacks on Palestinians—beatings, vandalizing homes, throwing stones, burning fields, killing livestock, and poisoning wells—as reprisals for attempts by Israeli officials to enforce Israeli law against the settlements.[6] Israeli law enforcement is generally lax when applied to Jewish perpetrators of violence or terrorism against Palestinian victims.

At the same time, there is reason for concern about the influence of rabbinical teaching on the conduct of Israeli military personnel. An analysis of publications circulated by the Israeli army rabbinate during Israel's winter 2008-09 Gaza offensive finds a "tone of nationalist propaganda that steps

Avigdor Lieberman was appointed to the post of Foreign Minister by Israeli Prime Minister Binyamin Netanyahu in early 2009. *Ha'aretz* journalist Gideon Levy lists the ideological similarities between the outlawed racist Kach Party founded in the 1970s by Rabbi Meir Kahane and the ultra-nationalist Yisrael Beitenu Party, founded in 1999 by Lieberman. "The differences," Levy warns, "are minuscule, not fundamental, and certainly not a matter of morality....Lieberman calls for a fascist 'test of loyalty' as a condition for granting citizenship to Israel's Arabs, while Kahane called for the unconditional annulment of their citizenship. One racist (Lieberman) calls for their transfer to the Palestinian state, the other (Kahane) called for their deportation."

Israeli Jewish residents of Bat Yam march on December 20, 2010, under the banner "Keeping Bat Yam Jewish" while chanting "Arabs out" and "No homes rented to Arabs." The rally followed the publication of a letter signed by dozens of Israeli municipal rabbis forbidding rentals to Arabs. The mayor of Bat Yam condemned the anti-Arab demonstrators' "shameful statements." Bat Yam is a city of 129,000 residents southwest of Tel Aviv.

blatantly into politics, sounds racist, and can be interpreted as a call to challenge international law when it comes to dealing with enemy civilians."[7]

Growing international opposition

In Cairo, on June 4, 2009, President Obama gave an historic speech addressed to the Muslim world. He reiterated that the bond between the US and Israel is "unbreakable," but declared with equal gravitas, "The situation for the Palestinian people is intolerable. And America will not turn our backs on the legitimate Palestinian aspiration for dignity, opportunity, and a state of their own." Obama's speech raised expectations of a change in US policy toward Islam and the Israel-Palestine conflict; those hopeful expectations are, to date, unmet.

On September 29, 2009, the UN Fact Finding Mission on the Gaza Conflict presented a 574-page document widely referred to as the Goldstone Report, which found that both the Israeli military and Hamas had committed war crimes and possibly crimes against humanity during the 2008-2009 Gaza war. Supporters of Israel's Gaza offensive claimed vindication when one of the report's four authors, Judge Richard Goldstone, published a partial recantation in an April 1, 2011, *Washington Post* op-ed.[8] Commenting approvingly on Israel's investigation of its own wartime conduct, Goldstone wrote, "it appears that an appropriate process is underway." Goldstone's rose-tinted assessment of Israel's capacity to investigate itself is starkly at odds with the findings of the Israeli human rights monitoring organization B'Tselem. In "Void of Responsibility," B'Tselem reports that

the Israeli military "effectively grants immunity to soldiers and officers, with the result that soldiers who kill Palestinians not taking part in hostilities are almost never held accountable for their misdeeds....Thus, the army allows soldiers and officers to violate the law, encourages a trigger-happy attitude, and shows gross disregard for human life."[9]

On April 1, 2009, General David Petraeus, addressed the US Senate Armed Services Committee, admitting that "Arab anger over the Palestinian question limits the strength and depth of US partnerships with governments and peoples [in the region]."[10] Petraeus's statement was widely interpreted to mean that the ongoing conflict in Israel puts the lives of American soldiers at risk.

International outrage flared on May 31, 2010, when the Israeli military staged a brutal attack on the Gaza Freedom Flotilla. Six ships carrying 750 peace activists from 40 different nations and thousands of tons of humanitarian supplies to Gaza were attacked in international waters 75 miles off the coast of Israel. Nine

> "They would have them stand, and there's the well-known Border Guard song (in Arabic): 'One hummus, one bean, I love the Border Guard' – they would make them sing this. Sing, and jump. Just like they do with recruits....The same thing only much worse. And if one of them would laugh, or if they would decide someone was laughing, they would punch him. Why did you laugh? Smack....It could go on for hours, depending on how bored they are. A shift is eight hours long; the time must be passed somehow."
>
> —Breaking the Silence testimony by Israeli border guard describing treatment of Palestinian detainees, YNet News (*Yedioth Ahronoth* online), January 29, 2010

people including one American on the Turkish ship *MV Mavi Marmara* were killed and over 50 were injured. A UN fact-finding mission wrote a detailed 56-page report concluding that Israeli forces committed "a series of violations of international law, including international humanitarian and human rights law."[11]

In early December 2010, 26 former European Union leaders sent a letter to top EU officials and member states condemning the open-ended nature of the US-brokered peace process. The signatories, which include the former EU foreign affairs chief, Javier Solana, Romano Prodi and Giuliano Amato of Italy, Richard von Weizsacker and

Breaking the Silence: Israeli soldiers' testimonies "dispel the darkess" surrounding wartime human rights violations

Occupation of the Territories—Israeli Soldier Testimonies 2000-2010, was published in December 2010 and contains almost 200 stories of men and women who have served in the Palestinian occupied territories. Dana Golan, executive director of Breaking the Silence, the Israeli veterans' organization that collected the testimonies, writes: "Examination of the last decade of Israeli presence in the Territories demonstrates the moral deterioration of Israeli society as a whole—not just that of its actors on the ground, the soldiers. We hope that

There had been no fire, no threat, nothing at all. Suddenly a shell is fired.

www.YouTube.com

(this) book...will stimulate a frank public debate on the moral price of ongoing control of another people."

Uri Avnery, a veteran of the Israeli peace community and a former Knesset member, sees something profoundly hopeful in the book's publication. "This generation understands its duty to heal the state in which they will spend their lives. In the words of the Hanukkah song, which is rapidly becoming the anthem of the anti-racist demonstrations: 'We come, the darkness to expel!'"

Israeli spokespersons defended the violent assault on the *Mavi Marmara* by Israeli commandos, but thousands turned out in international solidarity protests around the world to mourn the death of nine activists killed while attempting to break the illegal blockade of Gaza with a delivery of humanitarian relief and reconstruction supplies.

Helmut Schmid of Germany, Mary Robinson of Ireland, Felipe Gonzales of Spain, and Norway's Thorvald Stoltenberg, called for the imposition of firm deadlines and demands. In the absence of progress, the signatories recommended EU sanctions against Israel and a transfer of direction of the peace process from the United States to the United Nations.[12]

US-brokered peace talks fail

Shortly after Obama's Cairo speech in June 2009 his administration began putting pressure on Israel and the Palestinian Authority. The PA President Mahmoud Abbas responded: no negotiations until Israel freezes the construction of settlements on Palestinian land. In November Israeli Prime Minister Netanyahu declared a 10-month freeze but exempted "natural growth" in existing settlements as well as new construction in East Jerusalem. At the same time Israel's destruction of Palestinian homes in East Jerusalem increased. The peace talks went nowhere.

On the Israeli settlement issue, the US administration has suffered repeated public humiliation. On March 9, 2010, while Vice President Biden was in Jerusalem asserting the Obama administration's "absolute, total, unvarnished commitment to Israel's security," Prime Minister Netanyahu's office released an Interior Ministry announcement of 1,600 new housing units for Jews in East Jerusalem. This embarrassment to Vice President Biden only proved that US insistence on a settlement freeze had no teeth.

When the limited settlement-building freeze ended in September 2010, the biggest housing boom in a decade began throughout the occupied territories; by early 2011 two thousand housing units were under construction with 13,000 more in the pipeline. Finally, on December 7, 2010, the US abandoned efforts for a housing moratorium. On February 18, 2011, the US vetoed a UN Security Council resolution on the illegality of Israeli settlements, sending a clear message of abandonment to Palestinians (see sidebar, page 34).

International antagonism toward Israeli policy and uncritical US support for it will likely increase as US-Israeli intransigence is exposed as a primary barrier to resolution of the conflict. As of early 2011, 110 countries in the United Nations had granted diplomatic recognition to the State of Palestine—accepted internationally as the West Bank, East Jerusalem, and the Gaza Strip. The US is not among the nations recognizing Palestinian statehood. "Which leaves the United States, yet again, on the wrong side of history," according to Philip Giraldi, a former CIA officer and executive director of the Council for the National Interest.

The Palestine Papers

The fatal blow to the peace talks was delivered on January 23, 2011, when *The Guardian* and *Al-Jazeera TV* began releasing 1,600 secret documents on almost two decades of peace negotiations. These documents show that Palestinian leaders offered radical concessions for which they had no popular mandate: almost all of East Jerusalem; the refugee right of return (out of 4.6 million refugees, Saeb Erekat, chief Palestinian negotiator, demanded the return of only 1,000 refugees per year over a ten year period); the recognition of Israel as a Jewish state (meaning legalized inequality for non-Jewish citizens of Israel); abandonment of the 1967 borders; acceptance of the current configuration of isolated bantustans in the West Bank; and Israeli control over the Jordan Valley as well as the borders and the airspace of an eventual Palestinian state. Even with all these concessions, Israel rejected the Palestinian negotiators' offer, saying the package of compromises "does not meet our demands."[13] Jonathan Freedland of *The Guardian* observed that the Palestine Papers "blow apart what has been a staple of Israeli public diplomacy: the claim that [peace negotiations have failed because] there is no Palestinian partner."[14]

Others have observed that these Papers demonstrate just the opposite: that Palestinians have never had an Israeli peace partner. Israel's prolongation of a perpetual state of conflict gives Israel a free hand to delay defining its borders, grab more land, continue the process of ethnic cleansing, deepen the occupation, and continue the blockade of Gaza. Kathleen Christison, former CIA political analyst and author of several books on Palestine, writes that these papers reveal "US conduct throughout almost two decades of negotiations to be perhaps the most cynical, and indeed the most shameful, of the three parties'."[15]

As expected, the Palestine Papers have enraged the Palestinian people, shocked at their leaders' willingness to secretly sell out on inviolable principles. Palestinian chief negotiator Saeb Erekat resigned under popular pressure on February 12, 2011. Shortly after, the whole cabinet of the Palestinian Authority resigned and the PLO Executive Committee announced that elections for president and parliament would be held before October 2011. Hamas immediately announced it would not participate in the election nor recog-

On December 19, 2010, Human Rights Watch published a 166-page report titled *Separate and Unequal: Israel's Discriminatory Treatment of Palestinians in the Occupied Palestinian Territories.* The report shows that Israel operates a two-tier system for the two populations of the West Bank in the large areas where it exercises exclusive control. The report is based on case studies comparing Israel's starkly different treatment of settlements and next-door Palestinian communities in these areas. The HRW report calls on the US and EU member states and on businesses with operations in settlement areas to avoid supporting Israeli settlement policies that are inherently discriminatory and that violate international law.

nize its results, declaring the electoral procedure invalid, "because President Abbas (whose term of office expired in January 2009) has no legitimacy and is not fit to organize such elections."[16]

Revolution in Tunisia, Egypt,...and beyond?

Inspired by the Tunisian uprising in early January 2011 that forced the departure of that country's long-time autocratic leader, Zine el-Abidine Ben Ali, Egyptian demonstrators took to the streets on January 25 demanding regime change. Eighteen days later Egyptian President Hosni Mubarak was forced to vacate his post.

In Jordan, Bahrain, Yemen, Syria, Saudi Arabia, Libya, Morocco, and

Even as they resist and protest the Israeli occupation, Palestinians agitate for better leadership of their own. Here, thousands of Palestinians gather in Ramallah on March 15, 2011, to call for unity—an end to the Hamas–Fatah split—in their struggle for self-determination, human rights, and equality.

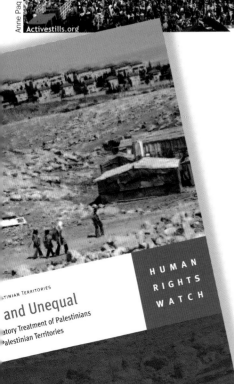

elsewhere in the region, demands for an end to autocratic rule and government repression have been expressed in diverse ways, drawing a variety of responses from government capitulation to brutal repression, as well as international intervention. Palestinian demonstrations in solidarity with the uprisings in North Africa and the Middle East have been violently repressed in the West Bank by the Palestinian Authority and in Gaza by Hamas, yet tens of thousands of Palestinian youth have defied the PA and Hamas, demanding an end to Palestinian political divisions.

The short-term and long-term outcomes of the popular uprisings in the Middle East remain to be seen. The world looks on with concern and cautious optimism, hopeful that the enormous sacrifices of the reform activists will be rewarded by the emergence of free societies led by representatives who are answerable to their people.

Hope in the midst of hopelessness

In their new Confession of Faith our Palestinian brothers and sisters in Christ "cry out from within the suffering in our country, under the Israeli occupation, *with a cry of hope in the absence of all hope*, a cry full of prayer and faith in a God ever vigilant, in God's divine providence for all the inhabitants of this land. Inspired by the mystery of God's love for all,...we proclaim our word...a word of faith, hope, and love." (Emphasis added) Two and a half decades of peace talks have brought only more land confiscation, settlement colonies, ethnic cleansing, apartheid, and humiliation for Palestinians. As Martin Luther King, Jr., reminded us, "We know through painful experience that freedom is never voluntarily given by the oppressor; it must be demanded by the oppressed." King also believed that "the arc of the moral universe is long, but it bends toward justice." Can we discern the hand of God in the changes now unfolding? Stay tuned.

Israelis turn out in large numbers to protest their government's implementation of policies designed to "Judaize" Arab sections of occupied East Jerusalem, as at this event held on June 25, 2010, in Silwan. Despite many inspiring cases of ongoing cooperation between Palestinians and Israelis, the evictions and house demolitions go on unabated, continuing a pattern of Palestinian dispossession as old as the Jewish state.

1   "New discriminatory laws and bills in Israel," Adalah, The Legal Center for Arab Minority Rights in Israel, November 29, 2010
2   Jonathan Lis, *Ha'aretz*, February 15, 2011
3   Email of January 7, 2011, from B'Tselem USA, "Israeli Knesset Investigation of Rights Groups: Reminiscent of America's McCarthyite Past"
4   "Preserve Israeli Democracy As We Know It," Rabbis for Human Rights–North America, February 8, 2011, www.rhrna.org/?p=1543
5   Jonah Mandel, *Jerusalem Post*, December 29, 2010
6   Jonathan Cook, August 2, 2010, www.counterpunch.org/cook08022010.html
7   Amos Harel, *Ha'aretz*, January 26, 2009
8   Richard Goldstone, "Reconsidering the Goldstone Report on Israel and war crimes," *Washington Post*, April 1, 2011
9   "Void of Responsibility," B'Tselem, October 2010, p. 6
10 http://armed-services.senate.gov/statemnt/2009/April/Petraeus%2004-01-09.pdf
11 www2.ohchr.org/english/bodies/hrcouncil/docs/15session/A.HRC.15.21_en.pdf
12 BBC News, December 10, 210, www.bbc.co.uk/news/world-middle-east-11968304
13 Donald Macintyre, *The Independent* (UK), January 24, 2011, www.independent.co.uk/news/world/middle-east/palestinians-ready-to-give-up-jerusalem-sites-2192667.html
14 Jonathan Freedland, *The Guardian*, January 23, 2011, www.guardian.co.uk/commentisfree/2011/jan/23/palestine-papers-israel-peace-partner
15 Kathleen Christison, January 25, 2011, www.counterpunch.org/christison01252011.html
16 Karl Vick, February 12, 2011, www.time.com/time/world/article/0,8599,2048790,00.html

Christian engagement for change

Mission in partnership

Presbyterians do mission in partnership!" This fundamental tenet of our denomination is particularly relevant in Palestine where our partners live under great stress. Partnership provides them with the ongoing encouragement that comes from knowing that fellow Christians around the world understand their situation and pray regularly for them.

We seek to "walk with" our partners: to learn from them, encourage them, and be guided in our actions by them. Staying in relationship can also equip the American partners with regular, up-to-date information as events unfold.

Our denomination has long-standing partnerships with various ecumenical bodies in Palestine: Episcopal, Lutheran, Orthodox, and Catholic; the Middle East Council of Churches (MECC); and other church and para-church organizations.

Many delegations explore our denomination's deep roots and long-term links with religious, educational, and health projects by meeting and worshiping with fellow Christians while they are there.

In Gaza, Presbyterian Disaster Assistance (PDA) works with Action by Churches Together (ACT), a global alliance of 175 churches and related organizations working worldwide to support communities in emergencies. The Department of Service to Palestinian Refugees of the MECC provides up-to-date information on the situation of Palestinian refugees in the

Partnerships in Israel/Palestine

- For further information about partnerships, see www.israelpalestinemissionnetwork.org/partnerships.

- A full list of our denomination's partners in Israel/Palestine can be found at www.pcusa.org/worldwide/israelpalestine/international.htm.

- To make a financial contribution through the denomination's Extra Commitment Opportunities (ECOs) in Israel and Palestine, go to www.pcusa.org/worldwide/israelpalestine/giving.htm.

- For gifts in response to emergency and crisis situations, go to www.pcusa.org/pda.

- For denominational guidelines for partnerships, see www.pcusa.org/worldwide/get-involved/protocols.htm.

- For advice on partnering in Israel/Palestine, contact Amgad Beblawi (amgad.beblawi@pcusa.org) or Sarah Humphrey (sarah.h.humphrey@gmail.com).

The International Center of Bethlehem started in 1994 with a budget of $327 as an outreach ministry of Christmas Lutheran Church. Since then, its exponential and inspirational growth has been due in part to committed partnerships with American Christians. Rev. Dr. Mitri Raheb, its general director, has overseen the growth of the Center's celebrated arts and crafts program.

David Young

Memorial PC, Midland, MI, has given strong support to the music program at Dar al-Kalima College at the International Center in Bethlehem, including support for a new practice building and a new music computer lab. They are providing scholarships for two students at the College's school of fine arts. Several people from the College have visited their church in Michigan; they hope to arrange a mission trip to Bethlehem soon. Contact Marilyn Wildes at marilynwildes@sbcglobal.net.

Donald Griggs

North Creek PC, Mill Creek, WA, is working with Bethlehem Bible College to help develop an Information Technology infrastructure to confront the pervasive economic hardships, enabling students to work in areas that provide IT employment. Contact: Joe Upton at peg.joe@verizon.net.

Lafayette-Orinda PC, Lafayette, CA, has visited and given strong support over the years to two organizations in Gaza: Ahli Arab Hospital and the Atfaluna Society for Deaf Children. They also participate in partnership with the Pilgrims of Ibillin in supporting the Mar Elias Educational Institutions and are faithful supporters of our Regional Liaison, Douglas Dicks. Contact: Tom Francis at thfrancis@deloitte.com.

Presbytery of Greater Atlanta. This presbytery's partnership, through the Presbyterian Hunger Program, is with a consortium of six church and para-church organizations in Palestine: the International Center in Bethlehem, Bethlehem Bible College, Wi'am, the YWCA, Democracy and Workers Rights Center in Ramallah, and the Palestine Working Women's Society for Development. For more information, contact Sarah Humphrey at sarah.h.humphrey@gmail.com).

Since 1999, **Philadelphia Presbytery** has had a partner-

Donald Griggs

Mar Elias Educational Institutions (MEEI) were found in Ibillin, Israel, by Elias Chacour (left), who is now th Archbishop for Galilee of the Melkite Catholic Church The school is known for academic excellence and a commitment to fostering interreligious and intercultural understanding. MEEI is one of the largest of educational high schools serving the Arab populatio in Israel, and more than 50% of its students are gir

ship with the Diocese of Jerusalem of the Episcopal Church of Jerusalem and the Middle East. The Presbytery has initiated many reciprocal visits with church partners in Palestine and Israel as well as in Jordan and Lebanon. Their members have been active participants in a nine-denomination Ecumenical Working Group for Middle East Peace, hosting conferences and workshops. Contact Rev. David Yeaworth (DandGYeaworth@verizon.net).

Keep Hope Alive is a Peacemaking program of three **San Francisco Bay Area Presbyteries and the UMC Task Force on**

David Young

Church-based iniatives for change

whole of Israel, the occupied territories, and Gaza.

Many Presbyterians travel to Israel and Palestine seeking to deepen their spiritual roots. Direct, personal experience builds awareness of the conflict that engulfs both Israelis and Palestinians. Upon returning home, they are anxious to learn more, share what they have learned, and influence the policies of our church and our nation. Many experience an irresistible urge to return to Israel/Palestine —and do.

Israel-Palestine, in partnership with the YMCA of East Jerusalem and the YWCA of Palestine. Each year, two delegations go to the West Bank to help Palestinian families plant olive trees (February) and harvest olives (October). Contact Walt Davis, waltandlibby@comcast.net.

Many congregations have ongoing links with the **Sabeel Ecumenical Liberation Theology Center** in Jerusalem, facilitated through **Friends of Sabeel North America** (www.fosna.org). This group frequently sponsors conferences in the US and in Palestine.

Other churches have links with **Mar Elias Educational Institutions** in Ibillin, Israel, established through the initiative of Archbishop Elias Chacour. These links are facilitated by the US organization, **Pilgrims of Ibillin** (www.pilgrimsofibillin.org).

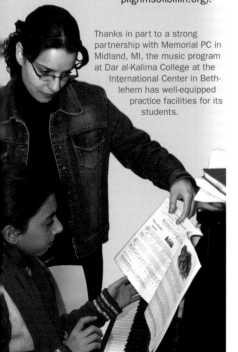

Thanks in part to a strong partnership with Memorial PC in Midland, MI, the music program at Dar al-Kalima College at the International Center in Bethlehem has well-equipped practice facilities for its students.

PC(USA) General Assembly statements from 1948 to 2003

Since 1948 Presbyterian General Assemblies have repeatedly addressed issues of relevance to the Middle East, particularly Israel and Palestine. Consistent with UN resolutions, the Church has affirmed the right of Israel to exist as a sovereign state within secure, internationally-recognized borders; affirmed the right of Palestinians to self-determination, including the right to the establishment of a viable, independent, sovereign state; and condemned acts of terrorism and other acts of violence against innocent people by all parties to the conflict.

The Assembly has also demanded an end to the occupation; a return to the pre-1967 borders (the "Green Line" set by the UN in 1949); the removal of all Israeli settlements on Palestinian land, or a one-for-one exchange of land; the removal of the Separation Barrier to the Israeli side of the border; the right of return of Palestinian refugees and their descendants and compensation for their losses; and an international Jerusalem shared by both Israel and Palestine.

PC(USA) General Assembly statements from 2004-2010

The 216th, 217th, 218th and 219th General Assemblies have struggled mightily with issues related to peace and justice in Israel and Palestine. This struggle can be best summarized by saying that the Presbyterian Church (U.S.A.) unequivocally stands for peace and justice in Israel/Palestine but is divided about how best to approach specific issues related to that goal. Our historical relationships with Palestinians, Israelis, and the American Jewish Community have complicated our attempts to speak with one prophetic voice. Following are highlights of General Assembly actions (all references to GA actions are from official Presbyterian website pages):

The 216th (2004) General Assembly directed the formation of a Palestine Mission Network "for the purpose of creating currents of wider and deeper Presbyterian involvement with Palestinian partners, aimed at demonstrating solidarity and changing the conditions that erode the humanity of Palestinians." That same decision also called for a "systematic effort of development and compassionate action in Palestine" providing the impetus for the network's activities related to travel, the marketing of Palestinian products, and seeking opportunities for pro-active investment in affordable housing and in other areas that contribute to economic improvement. The Assembly also called upon the Stated Clerk to issue a pastoral letter on Christian Zionism and on the ongoing conflict in Israel and Palestine, to post it on the PC(USA) website, and to "make known" the church's opposition to the construction of a wall and other barriers by the State of Israel in Occupied Palestinian Territory. The most controversial action that year was to refer to the Mission Responsibility Through Investment Committee (MRTI) "instructions to initiate a process of phased, selective divestment in multinational corporations operating in Israel, in accordance to General Assembly policy on social investing...."

The 217th (2006) General Assembly acknowledged the hurt and misunderstanding that occurred in the Jewish community as a result of actions taken by the 216th General Assembly and asked for "a new season of mutual understanding and dialogue." It also replaced the 2004 wording regarding divestment to assure that the financial resources of the church "be invested in only peaceful pursuits" and affirmed MRTI as the appropriate vehicle for achieving this goal. The Assembly also called upon the church to work for an end to all violence and terror against Palestinian and Israeli civilians; and, to work for an end to the occupation and toward the creation of a secure Palestinian state alongside a secure Israeli state.

In addition to the statements mentioned on page 3 of this resource, the 218th (2008) General Assembly directed GA offices to develop appropriate resources regarding Just Peace in Israel and Palestine; called for continued "corporate engagement with companies supporting or profiting from the occupation of Palestine and/or other violence in the region;" and called upon the church to "be a voice for the victims of violence and in both Israel and Palestine." Commissioners also called for the creation of a Middle East Study Committee to be appointed to study the conflict and bring back a comprehensive report to the 219th General Assembly.

The 219th (2010) General Assembly received, modified, and approved the comprehensive report of the Middle East Study Committee entitled "Breaking Down the Walls." Highlights of the recommended actions approved by passage of this report include calls for the end of Israeli occupation of Palestinian territories and diversion of water resources, an immediate freeze on illegal settlement building in Occupied Palestinian Territories (OPT), the relocation by Israel of the Separation Barrier to the 1967 border, the individual right of refugees to return or to adjudicate or negotiate compensation for the loss of home and homeland, reaffirmation of Israel's right to exist as a sovereign nation within secure and internationally recognized borders, and immediate cessation of all violence on both sides of the conflict. The report also condemned the business practices of Caterpillar, Inc., in the OPT, called upon the US government to make military aid to Israel contingent upon its ending human rights violations in the OPT, and commended *Kairos Palestine – A moment of truth* for study by the whole church, endorsing its emphases of hope for liberation, nonviolence, love for enemy, and reconciliation.

Kairos Palestine – A moment of truth

"Why now? Because today we have reached a dead end in the tragedy of the Palestinian people....The hearts of the faithful are filled with pain and with questioning: What is the international community doing? What are the political leaders in Palestine, in Israel, and in the Arab world doing? What is the Church doing? The problem is not just a political one. It is a policy in which human beings are destroyed, and this must be of concern to the Church.

Kairos Palestine is a contemporary, ecumenical confession of faith and call to action. It was launched in December 2009 by a group of Palestinian Christians and endorsed by the heads of churches in Palestine. Its tone and its theology echo similar Christian manifestos written in times of crisis, e.g., at the rise of Nazism (*Barmen Declaration*, 1934), during the civil rights movement in the US (*Letter from the Birmingham Jail*, 1963), and amidst the struggle to end Apartheid in South Africa (*Kairos Document*, 1985).

The 219th (2010) General Assembly of the Presbyterian Church (U.S.A.) "commends for study the *Kairos Palestine* document" and "endorses the document's emphases on hope for liberation, nonviolence, love of enemy, and reconciliation. We lift up for study the often neglected voice of Palestinian Christians."

What is the central message of *Kairos Palestine*? In the midst of "the absence of hope," Christian Palestinians proclaim a word of faith, hope, and love. At the same time they make the following declarations:

- The decades-old Israeli military occupation of Palestinian territories is a sin against God and humanity.

- Any theology or interpretation of the Bible by Christians or Jews that justifies this occupation is "far from Christian teachings."†

- Nonviolent resistance to this evil is "a right and a duty for all Palestinians, including Christians."

- "Human beings were not made for hatred." Only a resistance based on love of enemy and a repudiation of revenge can lead to a just peace and reconciliation.

Kairos Palestine also calls upon the Churches and the international community to join the nonviolent BDS movement (boycott, divestment, and sanctions) in taking economic, political, and diplomatic measures similar to those that led to the end of Apartheid in South Africa.

The memory of the *Nakba* (Arabic for "Catastrophe") shapes present-day consciousness and identity. As Americans learn about the Jewish and Palestinian "narratives," they also learn of Palestinian resentment about what they perceive as a double standard in the acceptance of their collective narrative. Palestinians observe that Jewish efforts to preserve the memory of their collective experience and *Shoah* (Hebrew for "Catastrophe") are met with respect and acceptance, while Palestinians are urged to "stop living in the past" and "move on."

Tamal Akham's painting (above) shows the expulsion of Palestinians through the port of Jaffa in 1948. Over 85,000 Palestinians living in Haifa and Jaffa at the time were forced to flee through the Mediterranean seaports. Some tried in desperation to escape on small fishing boats; those who found no place in the crowded boats were lost overboard.

† The use of the phrase "is far from Christian teachings" in the *Kairos* document appears to carry the same force as a charge of heresy.

The *Kairos Palestine* document is available as a 24-page booklet produced by the Israel/Palestine Mission Network of the PC(USA), paired with background information and a three-week study plan for group or individual use. Order item number 26466-10-001 at the Presbyterian Store online at http://store.pcusa.org or by calling 800.524.2612. You may also visit the *Kairos Palestine* website, www.kairospalestine.ps, for the document and additional information and resources.

Left: An Israeli affiliated with Anarchists Against the Wall walks hand in hand with a Kufr Qadum villager in a peaceful demonstration against encroachment by the nearby settlements Kedumim and Kedumim Ilit.

Left: Combatants for Peace is a group of former combat soldiers in the Israel Defense Forces and former fighters in the Palestinian liberation struggle. Today, these men share the belief that the conflict cannot be resolved through violence and occupation. In April 2009 a group of Israelis with the organization passed through Israeli checkpoints to enter the West Bank for a meeting and conversation with their Palestinian counterparts. (www.combatantsforpeace.org)

Yotam Ronen | Activestills

A tribute to Israeli peacemakers

Israeli activists are working creatively and courageously to foster the conditions for just peace. As ever-greater numbers of Israelis and Palestinians work together in nonviolent resistance to occupation, they are building the foundations for a future that embraces the interdependency of all who share the land. These photographs document the activities of only a few of the countless Israeli individuals and organizations from whose important work we draw inspiration and resolve.

Above: Israeli activists from Ta'ayush are sometimes present to intercede in cases of violence and harrassment against Palestinian villagers by settlers and soldiers in the rural South Hebron area. In July 2001 the shelters, fences, and baking ovens of five Palestinian villages in the area were demolished; then soldiers and civil administration workers poured debris into the wells that served as the villagers' only source of water. Since then Ta'ayush activists have led periodic convoys to bring food and water to the now-homeless Palestinians. (www.taayush.org)

Left: In January 2007 the acclaimed Israeli human rights organization B'Tselem launched its camera distribution project in the occupied territories. The camera enabled 14-year-old Fida' Abu 'Ayesha to capture on film numerous incidents of severe harassment in 2006 and 2007 perpetrated by extremist settlers who live in Tel Rumeida across the street from her house in Hebron. View it and others at www.btselem.org.

Don't you dare film me!

Below: Jeff Halper and Meir Margalit of the Israeli Committee Against House Demolitions attempt to prevent the demolition of a Palestinian home in Silwan, Jerusalem, in January 2008. (www.icahd.org)

ICAHD

Oren Ziv | Activestills

Below: Consisting of several hundred bereaved families, half of them Palestinian and half Israeli, the Parents Circle–Families Forum was founded in 1995 to foster reconciliation between Israelis and Palestinians beginning with its members—all of whom have lost immediate family members to the violence in the region. (www.theparentscircle.org)

Left: Israel is focused on uncovering the archaeological record of Jewish history as validation for its contemporary political claim. Since 1948 Israel's policies have deliberately erased and obscured the traces of the land's absent Palestinians. Zochrot ("Remembering" in Hebrew) is raising awareness among Israeli Jews of the history of Palestinians in the land. (www.zochrot.org)

די לכיבוש

די לכיבוש

Martha Reese

Right: MachsomWatch (machsom is Hebrew for "checkpoint") was founded in 2001 by Israeli women opposed to the Israeli occupation of the territories and the systematic repression of the Palestinians who live there. MachsomWatch members often take positions at checkpoints to monitor and attempt intervention in cases of abuse. MachsomWatch's videos on YouTube give a compelling insider's view of anti-occupation activism. (www.machsomwatch.org)

Keren Manor | Activestills

Above: In January 1988 a small group of Israeli women began a simple form of protest: once a week at the same time and place they donned black clothing and raised hand-shaped signs containing the message "Stop the Occupation." Now, Women In Black holds weekly vigils in Gan-Shmuel, Haifa, Jerusalem, Carmiel, Nachshon, Tel Aviv, and other cities around the globe.

A historical overview

Pre 1947—The Zionist beginnings

1897. First Zionist Conference meets in Basel, Switzerland, with goal of establishing a national Jewish homeland in historic Palestine where, at the time, Jews make up less than 2% of the population.

1914. The Ottoman Empire enters World War I on the side of Germany.

1917. Britain signs the Balfour Declaration supporting the "establishment in Palestine of a national home for the Jewish people...it being clearly understood that nothing shall be done which may prejudice the civil and religious rights of existing non-Jewish communities in Palestine...."

1918. World War I ends, bringing the defeat of the Ottoman Empire.

1920s. League of Nations grants Britain a mandate over Palestine and Jordan. Palestinian general labor strike and violent attacks protest Zionist immigration.

1939-47. Jewish immigration escalates in response to Nazi persecution and atrocities in Europe. In protest of British efforts to restrict immigration, Zionists organize underground gangs that attack British and Palestinian officials and civilians. Palestinian opposition to Zionism continues.

1947-1948—War of Independence and Arab cleansing

1947. The UN General Assembly passes Resolution 181, which would partition Palestine into Jewish and Arab states and establish Greater Jerusalem as an international city. The Jewish state would receive 56% of the land of the Palestine Mandate, the Arab state about 44%. Zionist leaders accept the plan; Palestinians reject it. Riots and fighting break out.

1948. Recognizing the impossibility of establishing a Jewish state in a land with a non-Jewish majority, Zionist forces launch a series of operations that induce the flight of some 750,000 Palestinians (75% of the indigenous Palestinian population). British withdraw as mandate ends. On May 14 Zionists declare Israel a Jewish State, and gain recognition by the United Nations. Egypt, Syria, Iraq, Lebanon, Jordan, and Saudi Arabia declare war on Israel. The war results in a divided Jerusalem and 531 "cleansed" Arab villages. Palestinian refugee camps are established in Lebanon, Syria, Jordan, Egypt, and in the areas now known as the West Bank and Gaza. In December the United Nations adopts the "Universal Declaration of Human Rights" and UN Resolution 194, stating that "refugees wishing to return to their homes and live at peace with their neighbors should be permitted to do so at the earliest practicable date, and those wishing not to return should be compensated for their property."

1949-1967—Consolidation

1949. Initial borders are established along what will become known as the Green Line, encompassing nearly 50% more territory into Israel than was originally allotted by the UN Partition Plan, a total of 78% of historic Palestine. West Bank and Gaza come under Jordanian and Egyptian control, respectively.

1953. Israel illegally begins to divert the waters of the Jordan River. In response President Eisenhower suspends all economic aid to Israel.

1964. The Palestine Liberation Organization (PLO) is established, advocating armed struggle for liberation.

1967. In a pre-emptive strike, Israel attacks Egypt, Syria, Iraq, and Jordan and in six days occupies the West Bank, Gaza, Sinai, Golan Heights, and the Arab sector of East Jerusalem. About 320,000 Palestinians are displaced, more than half of them for the second time. Israel immediately establishes Jewish-only settlements in the West Bank, Gaza, and East Jerusalem. In November the UN Security Council passes Resolution 242, stressing the "inadmissibility of the acquisition of territory by war" and calling for the "withdrawal of Israeli armed forces from territories occupied" and a "just settlement to the refugee problem."

1968-1992—Military occupation

1968-69. Fatah gains formal control of the PLO; Yassir Arafat becomes chair.

1973. On the Jewish holy day of Yom Kippur, Egypt and Syria attack Israel. With significant US economic and military assistance, Israel, although losing nearly 150 planes and suffering hundreds of casualties, pushes back both armies.

1974. The Arab League declares the PLO to be the only legitimate representative of the Palestinian people. The UN recognizes the Palestinians' right to sovereignty and grants observer status to the PLO.

1978. Egypt and Israel in the Camp David Accords reach a peace agreement, providing for the return of the Sinai to Egypt in exchange for recognition of Israel. Israel invades Lebanon, occupying its southern border in response to the violence of the PLO.

1980. Israel declares Jerusalem its eternal, undivided capital, affirming the 1967 annexation of East Jerusalem.

> "In Palestine we do not propose to go through the form of consulting the wishes of the present inhabitants....The four great powers are committed to Zionism and Zionism...is rooted in age-long tradition, in present needs, in future hopes, of far profounder import than the desires and prejudices of the 700,000 Arabs who now inhabit that ancient land.

—Lord Balfour, British Foreign Secretary, author of the Balfour Declaration, 1919

Yassir Arafat, shown here in a wall poster in Beirut's Sabra-Shatila refugee camps in 2003, led the Palestinian Liberation Organization from Jordan, Lebanon, and Tunisia until his return to Palestine in 1994 under a provision of the Oslo Accords. In late 2004, after being confined within his Ramallah compound for over two years by the Israeli army, Arafat died at the age of 75. Some remember Arafat as the tireless leader of the Palestinian struggle over decades, while others remember him as corrupt and inefficient, while still others think of him as a traitor and collaborator who sold out his people for personal legitimacy and financial gain. Since his death, Palestinian leadership has suffered from internal divisions and external pressures leading to political fragmentation.

1981. Israel annexes the Golan Heights.

1982. Israel invades Lebanon a second time, laying siege to Beirut. The PLO moves its headquarters to Tunis. Hezbollah (Party of God) comes into existence to counter the Israeli invasion. Beirut is occupied by Israel.

1982. Israeli troops under command of Ariel Sharon encircle the Sabra-Shatila Palestinian refugee camps in southern Beirut, allowing Lebanese Phalangist (Maronite Christian) troops to enter the camp and massacre thousands of women, children, and elderly men over a period of several days.

1983. Israel and Lebanon sign agreement terminating the state of war and recognizing the border. Arafat and PLO leadership, forced to leave, go to Tunis until 1994.

1985. The Israeli government orders the withdrawal of its troops from most of Lebanon. Israeli troops remain in southern Lebanon until 2000.

1987. The first Intifada, a Palestinian popular uprising, begins in Gaza and spreads to the West Bank. The uprising is crushed by Israelis.

1988. The PLO accepts UN Security Council Resolutions 242 and 338, implicitly recognizing Israel. The United States opens dialogue with the PLO. The Hamas Islamic Brotherhood is founded with a charter advocating the destruction of Israel.

1992. President George H. W. Bush's administration holds up ten billion dollars in US loan guarantees to Israel in an attempt to limit Israeli settlement building.

1993-2011—The 'Peace Process'

1993. Israel and the PLO sign the Oslo Declaration of Principles, which provide for mutual recognition. The PLO renounces violence and the use of terrorism and agrees to revise the PLO Charter to remove chapters referring to the destruction of Israel.

1994. A Jewish American settler in Hebron massacres 29 Palestinians praying in the mosque at the Tomb of the Patriarchs. Shortly thereafter the first Palestinian suicide bomber blows himself up inside Israel.

1994. The Palestinian National Authority (PNA) is established in Gaza and the West Bank. The PLO and Yassir Arafat arrive in Gaza. Jordan and Israel sign a peace treaty.

1995. Prime Minister Rabin is assassinated in Tel Aviv by an Israeli fundamentalist opposed to Oslo Accords.

1997. Israel starts building a settlement, Har Homa, on a hill overlooking East Jerusalem; widespread protests result. Israel imposes closures on Palestinian communities in the West Bank and Gaza.

2000. Israeli troops pull out of Lebanon. Israeli Prime Minister Ehud Barak, Palestinian Chairman Yassir Arafat, and US President Bill Clinton meet at Camp David in a failed attempt to negotiate a settlement on final status issues. The Al-Aqsa Intifada begins following a visit to the Temple Mount/Haram al-Sharif by Israeli opposition leader Ariel Sharon. The violence escalates rapidly and continues, involving rock-throwing, machine gun and mortar fire, suicide bombings, and road ambushes.

2001. Negotiations at Taba, Egypt, are unsuccessful.

2002. The Arab League (22 countries) proposes peace, normal relations, and regional integration with Israel in exchange for an end to the Occupation and a "just solution" to the refugee problem. Israel rejects the offer and begins unilateral construction of the Wall. In retaliation for a series of suicide bombings, the Israeli army reoccupies areas of the West Bank. Yassir Arafat is placed under house arrest.

2002-2003. The "Quartet" (US, UN, EU, Russia) develops "Roadmap to Peace." Palestinians pledge full support; Israel agrees but with 14 "reservations" that render it ineffective.

2004. Two Hamas leaders are killed in separate Israeli air strikes. Yassir Arafat dies.

2005. Israel evacuates 8,000 settlers from Gaza and constructs housing for 13,000 more settlers in the West Bank. Israeli troops withdraw from Gaza but retain control of crossings, airspace, and coastline.

2006. Hamas wins democratic legislative elections after holding to a unilateral ceasefire for more than a year. US and EU cut off aid and declare embargo on Palestinian government. Sharon suffers massive stroke, and Olmert assumes power. Gaza militants kill two Israeli soldiers and capture one; Israel launches a five-month attack on Gaza.

2007. Hamas and Fatah militants fight each other for control of Gaza. Annapolis Peace Conference launches unsuccessful one-year effort to achieve peace before the end of the Bush Administration.

2008-2009. Israel launches 22-day assault on Gaza. The official purpose, questioned by many Israelis, is to eradicate Hamas and stop rocket attacks.

2009. Likud Party chair Binyamin Netanyahu becomes prime minister of Israel, appoints Avigdor Lieberman deputy prime minister and minister of foreign affairs.

2011. Egyptian Revolution, January–February. Military government opens Rafah crossing at southern border of Gaza on Feb. 22 to two-way traffic.

Resources for further study

Many of the resources listed below were consulted in the preparation of this book. For a complete list of sources and citations used in this document, please visit IsraelPalestineMissionNetwork.org.

Books and Reports

Abunimah, Ali (2007) *One Country: A Bold Proposal To End the Israeli-Palestinian Impasse*

Amnesty International (June 2007) *Enduring Occupation, Palestinians Under Siege in the West Bank*

Ateek, Naim Stifan (2009) *A Palestinian Christian Cry for Reconciliation*

Aruri, Naseer (2003) *Dishonest Broker: The US Role in Israel and Palestine*

Baltzer, Anna (2007) *Witness in Palestine*

Bennis, Phyllis (2007) *Understanding the Palestinian-Israeli Conflict: A Primer*

Benvenisti, Meron (2002) *Sacred Landscape: The Buried History of the Holy Land since 1948*

Braverman, Mark (2010) *Fatal Embrace: Christians, Jews, and the Search for Peace in the Holy Land*

Burg, Avraham (2008) *The Holocaust Is Over; We Must Rise from Its Ashes*

Burge, Gary (2010) *Jesus and the Land: The New Testament Challenge to "Holy Land" Theology*

Carter, Jimmy (2006) *Palestine: Peace Not Apartheid*

Chacour, Elias (1984) *Blood Brothers*

Chacour, Elias (1990) *We Belong to the Land*

Chavits, Zev (2007) *A Match Made in Heaven*

Christison, Kathleen (2001) *Perceptions of Palestine: Their Influence on US Middle East Policy*

Cook, Jonathan (2008) *Disappearing Palestine: Israel's Experiments in Human Despair*

Curtiss, Richard H. (1990) *Stealth PACs: Lobbying Congress for Control of US Middle East Policy.* Washington, DC: The American Educational Trust

Marda Dunsky (2008) *Pens and Swords: How the American Mainstream Media Report the Israeli-Palestinian Conflict*

Ellis, Marc (1990) *Beyond Innocence and Redemption*

Findley, Paul (1993) *Deliberate Deceptions: Facing the Facts about the US-Israel Relationship* Washington, DC: The American Educational Trust

Findley, Paul (1985) *They Dare To Speak Out: People and Institutions Confront Israel's Lobby*

Gorenberg, Gershom (2006) *The Accidental Empire: Israel and the Birth of the Settlements, 1967-1977*

Grodzinsky, Yosef (2004) *In the Shadow of the Holocaust*

Halper, Jeff (2008) *An Israeli in Palestine*

Horowitz, Adam; Ratner, Lizzy; and Weiss, Philip, Eds. (2011) *The Goldstone Report*

Karpf, Anne et al. (2008) *A Time To Speak Out: Independent Jewish Voices on Israel, Zionism, and Jewish Identity*

Khalidi, Walid (1992) *All That Remains: The Palestinian Villages Occupied and Depopulated by Israel in 1948*

Mary Elizabeth King (2007) *A Quiet Revolution: The First Palestinian Intifada and Nonviolent Resistance*

Makdisi, Saree (2008) *Palestine Inside Out*

Mearsheimer, John L. and Walt, Stephen M. (2007) *The Israel Lobby and US Foreign Policy*

Miller, Aaron David (2008) *The Much Too Promised Land: America's Elusive Search for Arab-Israeli Peace*

Steadfast Hope, the companion DVD

This resource includes a DVD with nine segments.

- Chapter 1: Introduction: A Tale of Two Peoples (11 mins.)
- Chapter 2: The Big Picture (17 mins.)
- Chapter 3: Can We Call It Apartheid? (14 mins.)
- Chapter 4: Who Profits? (12 mins.)
- Chapter 5: Telling the Story (15 mins.)
- Chapter 6: Response: Theirs and Ours (15 mins.)
- Chapter 7: Middle East Uprisings (12 mins.)
- Chapter 8: Hardship and Hope (15 mins.)
- Chapter 9: Transformation (9 mins.)

The booklet and DVD can be used for individual learning and reflection, but, as with most curricula, participants will gain more if they are able to interact and share what they learn with others.

Steadfast Hope is available for purchase with its accompanying free DVD through the Presbyterian Church Store online http://store.pcusa.org or by phone 800-524-2612. Item number 26466-11-001.

Morris, Benny (1987) *The Birth of the Palestinian Refugee Problem, 1947-1949*

Nathan, Susan (2005) *The Other Side of Israel: My Journey Across the Jewish/Arab Divide*

Pappe, Ilan (2006) *The Ethnic Cleansing of Palestine*

Qumsiyeh, Mazin (2011) *Popular Resistance in Palestine: A History of Hope and Empowerment*

Said, Edward (2000) *Out of Place*

Sand, Shlomo (2009) *The Invention of the Jewish People*

Sharp, Jeremy M. (January 2008) "US Foreign Aid to Israel." Congressional Research Service Report for Congress, Prepared for members and committees of Congress

Shoshan, Malkit (2010) *Atlas of the Conflict: Israel-Palestine*

Sizer, Stephen (2007) *Zion's Christian Soldiers?*

Tolan, Sandy (2006) *The Lemon Tree: An Arab, A Jew, and the Heart of the Middle East*

Wagner, Don (2003) *Dying in the Land of Promise: Palestine and Palestinian Christianity from Pentecost to 2000*

Weber, Timothy P. (2004) *On the Road to Armageddon*

Zertal, Edith and Eldar, Akiva (2007) *Lords of the Land: The War over Israel's Settlements in the Occupied Territories*

Zunes, Stephen (2002) *Tinderbox: US Middle East Policy and the Roots of Terrorism*

Films and DVDs

Budrus (2010)

Cup Final (1991)

Jerusalem: The East Side Story (2008)

Miral (2010)

Occupation 101 (2007)

Paradise Now (2005)

Peace, Propaganda, and the Promised Land (2003)

Salt of This Sea (2008)

The Iron Wall (2006)

Witness in Palestine (2007)

A leader's guide to using this resource

Alvin Huie

Practical strategies for successful discussion leadership

Creating a space for open, safe conversation occurs as you set the tone by being a non-anxious presence and example for those present. *Remember that the tenor of the first encounter sets the stage for those that follow.*

Be clear with your participants about the amount of time you expect to be together. Your role as the presenter and leader means that you may act as a moderator if participants too quickly take sides in the conversation. You may also wish to be specific about your expectations for honorable speech with one another in claiming one's own positions and responding to the readings.

Make sure that everyone gets to share before others share for a second time. Be sure to preserve time for your group to process what they have seen

Keep Hope Alive is a Peacemaking program of three San Francisco Bay Area Presbyteries and the UMC Task Force on Israel-Palestine, in partnership with the YMCA of East Jerusalem and the YWCA of Palestine. Each year, two delegations go to the West Bank to help Palestinian families plant olive trees (February) and harvest olives (October). The presence of internationals can help Palestinians avoid confrontation with armed Israeli settlers who seek to prevent the Palestinians' planting and harvesting on their land, thereby depriving Palestinians of their primary source of income.

and consider what it is God may be calling them to do with what they are learning. Because of the amount of material there is to cover , it is

essential to give participants time to process the information thoughtfully. For that reason, the seven-week format described in the box on this page is highly recommended.

Make sure you have a comfortable space for the presentation and conversation where all can see and hear who is speaking. If you are able, display a large post-1967 map of Israel/Palestine to help in identifying the places discussed in the materials. Finally, painful experience teaches that it is always wise to test your DVD player and screen ahead of each class.

The three-part meeting format works well in studying challenging or controversial material:

1. Begin by recognizing God's presence in your midst with a prayer. Depending on your group, it may be necessary to set the stage for a time of conversation and sharing by providing a 15- to 20-minute overview of the range of materials. This can be accomplished by a combination of the DVD visuals provided and a spoken overview of the reading that has been assigned. This practice is especially helpful for those who may have done their reading weeks before and those catching up with the conversation.

Planning to lead a study-discussion group in your church

This book and the accompanying free DVD are designed for individual use or within a multi-week church adult education curriculum.

Seven-week series (recommended)

Week	Theme	Booklet	DVD
1	Mandate for Peacemaking	Pages 1–8	Chapter 1 (11 mins.)
2	Perspective	Pages 9–14	Chapter 2 (17 mins.)
3	Is it apartheid?	Pages 17–29	Chapter 3 (14 mins.)
4	Who Profits?	Pages 32–35	Chapter 4 (12 mins.)
5	Telling the Story	Pages 15–16	Chapter 5 (15 mins.)
6	Response & Looking Ahead	Pages 30–31, 36–39	Chapters 6, 7 (27 mins.)
7	Hardship & Hope	Pages 17–29, 40–43	Chapters 8, 9 (24 mins.)

Four-week series

Week	Theme	Booklet	DVD
1	Mandate for Peacemaking	Pages 1–14	Chapters 1, 2 (28 mins.)
2	Living with Occupation	Pages 17–31	Chapters 3, 8 (29 mins.)
3	Profits & Press	Pages 15–16, 33–35	Chapters 4, 5 (27 mins.)
4	Response & Looking Ahead	Pages 36–43	Chapters 6, 7, 9 (36 mins.)

One-week conversation

Hand out copies of the booklet and DVD one to two weeks in advance so participants have enough time to watch the DVD as a feature film and read through the entire 48-page booklet. Because of time limitations, you will have to decide what part of the booklet to emphasize. Chapter 2 of the DVD, "The Big Picture," is recommended. You can use the three-part meeting format described on pages 47-48 or tailor your time together based on the level of exposure your participants have on this topic.

2. Next, elicit from the participants what was new or surprising to them in the materials and presentation. This will help you locate where the participants are in their understanding of the issues. Don't underestimate the power of this step as the more introverted participants may take a while longer than the extroverted ones to feel safe sharing their voice and thoughts with the group.

3. Finally, offer some "digging deeper" questions, such as those suggested on the next page. If you feel at ease with the materials and topic, it may be tempting to begin answering the questions at this point. Instead, see if you can draw out differing responses from the members of your group. Remember, you are trying to provide a safe space for the participants to hear the resource and each other, with the hope that they will be ready to respond in the way the Holy Spirit invites. Finish with the assignment for the next week and a closing prayer.

As with other topics of exploration, the Israeli-Palestinian conflict can bring out strong feelings and reac-

"Digging deeper" questions to encourage productive group discussion

- What is your narrative of the Israeli-Palestinian conflict. Why?

- What does peacemaking mean to you?

- Is it easy for you to take sides in armed conflicts. Why, or why not?

- Some would say that this conflict is too complex to understand fully. In what ways is it simple to understand?

- How is the voice of the American media consistent or divergent from what has been presented in this study?

- How does the religious and ethnic diversity in Israel/Palestine hinder or aid the prospect for peace?

- What does the holy city of Jerusalem mean to you as a Christian? To Jews? To Muslims? To local Christians in Palestine/Israel?

- How does seeing the Israeli-Palestinian conflict as a recent phenomenon, rather than as an ancient religious conflict, help give you hope that peace is possible?

- What is the closest metaphor for the settlements in modern history?

- What would you do if you were cut off from a portion of your county or state and could not get to school, work, or civic events?

- What would you do if civilians in a neighboring country were being targeted by armed forces?

- What natural resources do you take for granted? What would you do if you were no longer granted access to those resources?

- For you, is physically violent resistance to injustice ever permissible?

- What will need to happen for a just peace to come about between Palestinians and Israelis?

- Do you profit through injustice in any of your investments? How do you know?

- In light of what you have learned through this study about what others are doing, what can you and your congregation do?

tions. The Peacemaking Program has multiple resources that help congregations with such conversations, including "To Strengthen Christ's Body: Tools for Talking about Tough Issues" (PDS Item #2435808001).

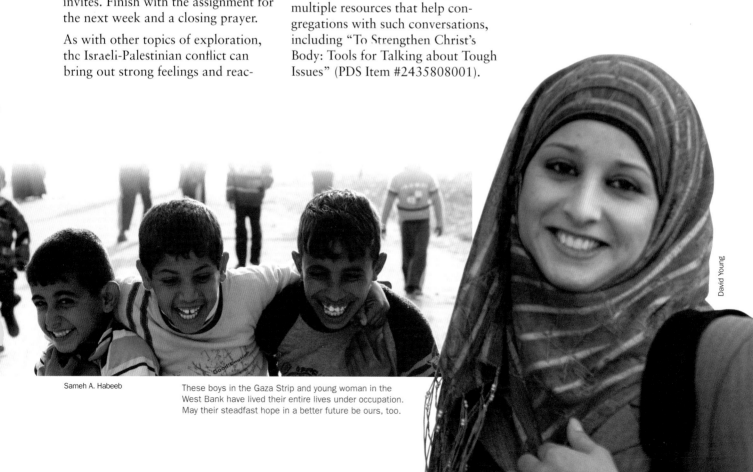

Sameh A. Habeeb

These boys in the Gaza Strip and young woman in the West Bank have lived their entire lives under occupation. May their steadfast hope in a better future be ours, too.

David Young